7-19-02

A PLAYDATE WITH DEATH

A PLAYDATE WITH DEATH

Ayelet Waldman

BERKLEY PRIME CRIME, NEW YORK

A PLAYDATE WITH DEATH

A Berkley Prime Crime Book
Published by The Berkley Publishing Group,
a division of Penguin Putnam Inc.,
375 Hudson Street, New York, New York 10014.

Visit our website at
www.penguinputnam.com

First edition: June 2002

Library of Congress Cataloging-in-Publication Data

Waldman, Ayelet.
    A playdate with death / Ayelet Waldman.— 1st ed.
    p. cm.
    ISBN 0-425-18473-0 (pbk.)
    I. Title.

PS3573.A42124 P58 2002
813'.54—dc21

                                          2001059239

PRINTED IN THE UNITED STATES OF AMERICA

10   9   8   7   6   5   4   3   2   1

To Sophie, Zeke, and Ida-Rose

Acknowledgments

MANY thanks go to Susanna Praetzel who gave me critical information about Tay-Sachs disease; to Julie Barroukh, Sandra Braverman, Lauren Cuthbert, Ginny Dorris, Clare Duffy, Allison Kaplan Sommer, Carlie Masters William, Saundra Schwartz, and Karen Zivan for being ever-present companions and ever-useful sources of information; to Mary Evans, Jeff Frankel, and Sylvie Rabineau for working so tirelessly on my behalf; to Sue Grafton, an inspiration and a role model; and to Michael, my best friend.

One

ISAAC shot me two times in the chest. With his toast.

"You're dead," my two-and-a-half-year-old son said, biting off a chunk of his Glock 9mm semiautomatic pistol.

"Mama doesn't like that game, Isaac. You know that. Mama doesn't like guns." I ruffled his hair with my hand, planted a kiss on the top of his older sister's head, and turned to my husband. "Don't cut his bread on the diagonal anymore."

"Why not?" Peter asked over the top of his coffee mug. His hair stuck out in wiry spikes and his gray eyes were bleary with exhaustion.

"Because he chews out the middle and turns the crust into a gun."

"Maybe if he had a *toy* gun, he wouldn't need to fashion weapons out of his *breakfast*."

I gave my husband a baleful glare and poured my own coffee. I leaned against the kitchen table and slurped. Ruby turned to me with a conspiratorial air made only slightly ridiculous by the fact that her uncombed curls stood up all over her head. She looked like a dandelion puff.

"Isaac has been playing guns all morning, Mama. And Daddy let him."

"Oh really?" I said.

"Don't be a tattletale, Ruby," Peter said.

He was right. Telling tales is a dreadful habit. Nonetheless, I was glad of an ally. I was becoming heartily sick of Isaac's never-ending game of "bang bang you're dead." Honestly, what *is* it with boys? Before I had one of my own, I would have sworn up and down that gender differences were cultural constructs and that it was possible to raise a boy who defied stereotypes by being more interested in dolls than trucks and in arts and crafts than weapons. Then Isaac was born. And he *was* interested in dolls: Superman dolls. Batman dolls. And he *loved* painting and sculpture; they were wonderful tools with which to make the weapons I wouldn't buy for him.

I took away the Play-Doh, the modeling clay, and all cylindrical objects. We stopped eating food that could be easily chewed into the shape of artillery. I banned all remotely aggressive videos and television, including most of the Disney movies the kids liked; Peter Pan spends way too much time sword-fighting and that Sea Witch would inspire anyone to violence. I refused to be swayed by the fact that Isaac was chafing under a diet of *Teletubbies* and *Barney*.

Mindless pap was better than warfare any day. I bought him a succession of gender-neutral toys and videos, played house with him, changed his dolls' diapers, and taught him every single Pete Seeger song I could remember. So far, my efforts had borne exactly no fruit.

My mother attributed Isaac's gun obsession to the fact that I'd been shot the day I gave birth to him, but that's just blaming the victim, as far as I'm concerned.

"What fabulous thing are you guys going to do today?" I asked. I'm afraid I didn't do a terribly good job of concealing my glee at the thought of being excluded from my family's plans for the morning. Peter, a screenwriter, had just finished two long months of shooting on his latest work of art, *The Cannibal's Vacation.* The director had demanded his presence on the set, apparently worried that without Peter there to rewrite various exclamations of horror, the film would never wrap. To compensate me for having been alone with the kids while he lounged away the days and nights on Lomboc, a lesser-known tropical island in Indonesia, my husband had been doing solo kid duty for a week or so.

"We're going fishing for dinosaurs," Isaac announced.

"Really?" I asked.

"We are *not* going fishing." Ruby reached across the table and pinched her brother, who squealed in protest. I inserted myself between them and frowned at her.

"Ruby, watch it, or you won't be going anywhere," I said.

"Yes I will. Because Daddy promised to take us to the La Brea Tar Pits, and you're going to the gym, so I am *too* going."

The mouth on that kid. But you couldn't argue with her logic.

I didn't bother answering her, just picked Isaac up and buzzed him with my lips. "I'm going to miss you guys today," I lied.

"You could come if you want." Peter's voice was a hopeful squawk.

"No thanks. Ruby's right, I'm going to the gym."

I plopped Isaac on the floor and finished my coffee with a gulp. I took a Powerbar out of my stash hidden in the back of the pantry, waved gaily at my family, and headed out the door.

"I'm taking your car!" I shouted, all too happy to leave Peter with my station wagon bursting with car seats, baby wipes and broken toys, and haunted by a mysterious odor whose origin lay in some long-lost tube of fluorescent yogurt. I slipped into his pristine, orange, vintage BMW 2002, popped the car into gear, and zipped off down the street, reveling in my hard-won freedom.

I'm the first to admit that I'm a somewhat unwilling stay-at-home mom. Not that I didn't choose the role. I did. Before I'd had my kids, I'd been a public defender representing indigent criminals in federal court. My particular specialties had been drug dealers and bank robbers, but I'd happily handled white-collar cases and even the odd assault on a national park ranger. I had never expected to leave work. I'd planned for a three-month maternity leave, imagining that I'd toss Peter the baby to take care of while I happily continued my twelve-hour-a-day schedule. I even tried it after

Ruby was born. I went back to work when she was four months old, skipping off with my breast pump in one hand and my briefcase in the other. Ten months later, I was back home. I couldn't stand being away from her for so much of the time. By the time I realized that I wasn't any happier at home all day than I'd been at work all day, I was already pregnant with Isaac. That pretty much put the nails into my professional coffin. The past couple of years had passed in something of a blur, punctuated by car pool, endless loads of very small laundry, and the occasional murder.

I pulled into the parking lot of my gym and slipped into a spot. For my last birthday, Peter had given me a series of training sessions at a glitzy Hollywood health club. I had decided to view the gift not as a passive-aggressive comment on the magnitude of my ass but rather as the expression of a good-hearted wish to see me fit and healthy. I'd been having a terrific time, despite my usual loathing of all things physically active. There is something remarkably pleasurable about having your very own personal trainer hovering over you, expressing apparently sincere interest in your food intake and exercise concerns. I, like the majority of women I know, am certain that the rest of the world finds every detail of my calorie neuroses and body image obsession as scintillating as I do myself. I skipped into the gym, ready to confess to Bobby Katz the grim tale of the four Girl Scout cookies and half pound of saltwater taffy I'd eaten the night before.

Instead of the collection of almost familiar Hollywood faces in brightly colored Lycra, straining under Cybex machines and hefting free weights, I found an empty gym. There were no trainers shouting encouragement, no beautifully sculpted and perfectly made-up starlets grunting and groaning. The machines glinted forlornly in the sun shining through the windows, and the place echoed with a silence made all the eerier because I'd never before walked in without being subject to a blaring retro-disco beat.

It took me a few minutes to track down the denizens of my snazzy workout studio. They were huddled around the juice bar behind the locker rooms. The trainers, deltoids shining with carefully applied moisturizer and abdominal six-packs peeking from skintight tops cropped at the midriff, wept noisily. The clientele, a bit more concerned with the exigencies of eye makeup and foundation, dabbed their eyes with Kleenex. The owner of the gym, an oversized Vietnamese bodybuilder named Laurence, opened his arms to me and pressed me to his sweaty chest.

"Oh darling. You poor darling. You don't even know, do you? You just came here to see him, and you don't even *know*," he wailed.

"Laurence, calm down. Tell me what's happened," I said as I attempted to extricate myself from his damp embrace. His nipple ring was poking me in the cheek.

"It's *Bobby*. He's *dead*. They found him this morning in his *car*. He *shot* himself."

I gasped, and now leaned against Laurence despite myself. "What? What are you talking about?"

"Betsy just called. He didn't come home last night, so she called the cops. They found his car parked on the PCH, just north of Santa Monica. Bobby was inside. Dead. He shot himself in the head."

I led Laurence over to a stool and sat him down. Then I asked him, "How's Betsy?"

"She's a mess, of course. Oh my God, I can't stand this, I can't *stand* this," Laurence wailed, burying his face in his hands.

"Oh for God's sake, Laurence. Quit crying. This is not *your* opera, girlfriend." I turned to Jamal Watson, one of the other trainers. He was dressed, as usual, in a vibrant shade of pink. His dark-brown leg muscles strained at his micro-mini shorts, and his top stopped a good six inches above his bellybutton. He looked back at me and said somewhat abashedly, "I mean, really, Bobby was my friend, too. Laurence here is acting like he's the only one who's devastated. We all are."

I turned back to the weeping gym owner. "Laurence, honey. You're upset. You should close up shop for the day." The other trainers and clients began to protest. They were sad, very sad, but not quite sad enough to sacrifice a morning's worth of crunches and leg lifts.

"No. No." Laurence heaved himself off his stool with a sigh. "The show must go on. Back to work, all of you. Back to work. That's what Bobby would have wanted." He waved everyone onto the gym floor and turned back to me. "Shall I give you a referral? Luzette's got some free slots, I think."

"No, no, that's okay. Maybe later. Can you give me Betsy's address? I want to see if she needs some help or if she could use a shoulder to cry on."

I could have used one myself. I'd been working out with Bobby Katz only for about six months, but in that short period of time, we'd gotten strangely close. Or maybe it wasn't so strange, considering the fact that we spent three hours a week together, most of that time filled with intimate conversations about our lives, loves, and the shape of my thighs. As a teenager, Bobby had made the thirty-mile leap from Thousand Oaks in the Valley to Hollywood, convinced that his sparkling azure eyes, flaxen hair, and laser-whitened teeth would garner him instant fame. It hadn't taken him long to realize that there were at least 7,200 other kids who looked just like him auditioning for all the same parts. He'd had some success. He'd gotten a couple of fast-food commercials and even a role in an Andrew Dice Clay movie. Unfortunately, his part in that work of cinematic genius was so small it could only be appreciated using the frame-by-frame viewing feature of a VCR.

He'd become a personal trainer as a way to supplement his acting income; it had soon become his career. And if I'm anything to go by, Bobby was good at what he did. I'd gained over sixty pounds with my second pregnancy, and despite the fact that Isaac was now well over two years old, before I met Bobby, I hadn't managed to lose more than half of it. He'd put me on a kooky diet that involved eating a lot of egg-white omelets and set me on a workout program that was having remarkable results. I could actually see my feet if I looked down. And craned my neck. And leaned a bit forward. Anyway, it was working for me. But that's not why I kept coming back. Before Bobby, I'd quit every exercise regime I'd ever begun, despite the fact that they all showed at least some results. I kept seeing Bobby because I liked him. He was a sweet, gentle man with a ready hug and an arsenal of delightfully dishy Hollywood gossip. He remembered everything I told him and seemed genuinely to care about what I'd done over the weekend or how Isaac's potty training was progressing. He was interested and attentive without being remotely on the make. He gave me utterly platonic and absolutely focused male attention.

A few months before that horrible morning, Bobby had asked for my advice as a criminal defense lawyer. He was a recovered drug user and an active member of Narcotics Anonymous, where he'd met his fiancée Betsy, and he'd asked me for help on her behalf. She'd fallen off the wagon and tried to make a buy from an undercover cop. The good news was that she never actually got the drugs. The bad news was that she found herself in county jail. I was thrilled at the opportunity to help Bobby after all he'd done for me, and I'd gotten them in touch with a good friend of mine from the federal public defender's office who had recently hung out her own shingle. Last I'd heard, Betsy's case had been referred to the diversion program. If she remained clean for a year and kept up with NA, it would disappear from her record.

Betsy and Bobby's place was in Hollywood, not too far from my own duplex in Hancock Park. I gave a little shudder as I climbed the rickety outdoor staircase up to their apartment. The building was made of crumbling stucco held together with rotted metal braces. The doors of each unit were dented metal, spray painted puce. The floor tile in the hallway was cracked, and large chunks were missing. Given the Los Angeles real estate market, they probably paid at least fifteen hundred a month to live in this dump.

Betsy opened the door and fell into my arms, a somewhat awkward endeavor since she was at least six inches taller than I. I led her inside and found myself face-to-face with two police officers. The cops took up much more space than it seemed they should have. The instruments hooked on to their black leather belts—the guns, billy clubs, radios, and other accoutrements of the LAPD—seemed to blow them up all out of human proportion. They were planted on the electric green carpet like a couple of bulls in a too-small pasture. I squeezed by one of the pneumatically enlarged officers and lowered Betsy onto the light beige leather couch, where she folded in on herself like a crumpled tissue.

I turned back to the men. "I'm Juliet Applebaum. I'm a friend of Betsy and Bobby's."

One of the officers, a man in his late twenties with a buzz cut so short and so new that his ears and neck looked raw, nodded curtly. "We're here to escort Betsy on down to the station so she can give a statement."

I turned to the weeping girl. "Betsy, honey? Do you want to go with the officers?"

She shook her head, buried her face in her hands, and slumped over on the couch.

"I don't think Betsy's quite ready for that," I said in a firm voice.

The officer shook his head and, ignoring me, leaned over

Betsy's prone form. "It'll just take a few minutes. The detectives are waiting for you." He managed to sound both menacing and polite at the same time.

Betsy just cried harder and jerked her arm away from the officer's extended hand. I sat down next to her and slipped an arm around her shoulders.

"Officer, why don't you let the detectives know that Betsy's just too distraught right now." The cop started to shake his head, but I interrupted him. "Am I to understand that you are placing her under arrest?" I asked. I felt Betsy quiver under my arm, and I gave her back a reassuring pat.

"No, no, nothing like that," the other officer spoke up. He looked a bit older than the one trying to get Betsy up off the couch. "We just need her to give a statement to the detectives."

"Unless you're planning on arresting her, Betsy's going to stay home for now. You can let the detectives know that they can contact her here. And if there's nothing further, I think Betsy would like to be left alone."

The police officers looked at each other for a moment, and then the older one shrugged his shoulders. They walked out the door, leaving behind a room that suddenly seemed to quadruple in size.

I patted Betsy on the back for a while, and then got up to make some tea. Bobby had introduced me to the wonders of green tea, and I could think of no time when I'd needed a restorative cup of Silver Needle Jasmine more than at this moment. I opened the fridge in the little galley kitchen off the living room and sorted through the jars of protein powder and murky green bottles of wheat grass juice until I found a little black canister of tea. I dug up a teapot and ran the faucet until it was hot. I poured some water over the leaves and let them steep for a moment. By the time I came back out to the living room holding two small cups of tea, Betsy had gathered herself together and was wiping her eyes and blowing her nose.

"Thanks," she said. "You still know how to be a lawyer."

"What? Making tea?"

"No, no." She smiled through her tears. "Getting rid of the cops."

"Don't mention it. Pissing off cops is my specialty. Are Bobby's parents on their way?"

Betsy shook her head.

"Do they know?"

She nodded and said, "The police called them this morning and told them. I tried to call, too, but they aren't answering the phone. I just keep getting the machine."

That surprised me. "You mean you haven't talked to them at all?"

"I haven't talked to them in months. Ever since . . . ever since that whole thing happened. When they found out about it, they tried to get Bobby to break up with me. They told him that I was a bad influence and that I'd drag him down. Which I guess I did." The last was said in a sort of moan, and more tears dripped down her cheeks.

I wrapped my arm around her and handed her a tissue and the cup of tea. "Drink," I said. "It'll make you feel better." She took a few sips and then blew her nose loudly.

"You weren't a bad influence on Bobby," I said, although I have to admit that at the time of her arrest, I'd taken the same line as Bobby's parents, albeit a bit more delicately. I'd just suggested to Bobby that since he had worked so hard to kick his addiction, he might want to put a little distance between himself and Betsy, just until she got her act together. Bobby had thanked me for my advice and gently informed me that he loved Betsy and planned to stand by her. I'd been chastened and never mentioned my reservations again. I had still had them, though. Bobby was the poster child for twelve-step programs. He'd stopped using methamphetamine five years before and hadn't missed a weekly meeting since. Before he'd gotten sober, his addiction was so bad that it was costing him hundreds of dollars a week, just to stay awake. He'd turned his athlete's body into a husk of its former self. The damage he'd caused to his heart from years of drug abuse was permanent. Despite the great shape he'd managed to return himself to, he still had an enlarged heart and a severe arrhythmia. Bobby had once told me that methamphetamine was so toxic to him nowadays that even holding the stuff and having it absorb through his fingers could trigger a heart attack. The risks to him of falling off the wagon were astronomical. I'd been terribly worried that Betsy's weakness would be contagious. But, in the end, he'd proven me wrong. He'd gotten her back on the program and never fallen off himself. So I had believed, until that morning.

"Betsy, why were the police here? Did they tell you why they need you to make a statement?"

"No. They just said I have to."

"But it's a suicide, right? Bobby killed himself?"

"I don't know. I mean, that's what they told me this morning. They said they found him in the car with a gun in his hand, and that he'd shot himself in the head."

"Was it his gun?"

She shook her head. "I don't think so. I mean, he doesn't have a gun. At least I don't think he does."

"And just now, when the cops were here, did they tell you they were considering other things? Like maybe that someone had killed him?"

She sniffed loudly and wiped her nose on her sleeve. "They didn't tell me anything."

"Betsy, do you think Bobby killed himself?" I asked flat out.

She shook her head and wailed, "I don't know. None of this makes any sense. I mean, why would he kill himself?"

"I don't know," I said. "But then, I don't know him as well as you do. Had anything happened between you two? Had you guys been getting along?" The truth was, I didn't expect Betsy to confide in me. I didn't know her that well, and for all I knew, Bobby had told her that, like his parents, I'd encouraged him to break up with her.

"Things were great. Great," she said firmly, rubbing the tears away from her eyes. "We'd set a date for the wedding; we'd even picked a rabbi."

"A rabbi? But you're not Jewish, are you?"

"Bobby's parents really wanted us to have a rabbi. Their

guy said that he'd do it, if we went to premarital counseling and if Bobby did all the tests and stuff."

"Tests?"

"Yeah, you know. Genetic testing for Tay-Sachs. The rabbi says he makes all Jews who he marries get Tay-Sachs testing. Just in case."

Tay-Sachs disease is a birth defect that is carried by something like one in thirty Jews of European descent. If two carriers have children together, they have a one in four chance of giving birth to a baby who will die of Tay-Sachs. Tay-Sachs is always fatal; generally, children die by age five after being desperately ill for most of their lives. Nowadays, there's a simple blood test to determine if you are a carrier. Most Jewish couples automatically gets tested, but Peter and I hadn't bothered, since Peter wasn't Jewish. Both of us would have had to be carriers for there to be any danger, so we'd never even considered it.

"Bobby had it," Betsy said.

"Had it? You mean Tay-Sachs? He was a carrier?"

"Yeah. We found out a few months ago, right before my . . . my arrest. I mean, it's no big deal that he had it, because of course I don't have it since I'm not Jewish. I mean, it *wasn't* a big deal." She sniffed. "I guess none of that matters anymore."

I didn't answer.

"What am I going to do?" she asked, turning to me and peering into my eyes.

I shook my head helplessly. "I don't know, Betsy. Get through every day, one day at a time, I guess."

"One day at a time? You sound like my goddamn spon-sor," she said. "You sound like Bobby."

I sat with Betsy for a while longer, leaving only when her Narcotics Anonymous sponsor and a few other friends from the group arrived.

Two

WHEN I got home from Betsy's, I found my kids and my husband hurling themselves around the living room wearing pink tutus; Peter's was around his neck. Ruby had a collection of tulle, lace, and ribbon that rivaled that of the Joffrey Ballet. From the moment she was able to make her sartorial preferences known, she'd begun lobbying for frills and ruffles. If she'd had her own way, she'd have had a pastel-colored confirmation gown for every day of the week. We compromised on cute little patterned cotton dresses and a costume box fit for a drag queen.

As soon as Isaac was born, she'd begun stuffing him into leotards and draping feather boas around his neck. He was only too glad to oblige his idolized older sister and happily participated in her endless stage productions and ballet recitals. Lately, he'd begun adding his own accessories, and it was not uncommon to find him, as I did that day, wearing a pink tutu, a purple ostrich feather tucked behind his ear, and a sword and scabbard belted around his waist.

"Mama! I'm a Princess Knight," he announced. Then he whipped out his sword and clocked his sister on the head with it.

"Damn it, Peter, I put that sword away for this very reason. Why did you take it out?" I said.

"Because you can't be a Princess Knight without a sword."

"Why does he have to be a Princess *Knight*? Why can't he just be a princess? Or a prince? A nice prince. Who kisses the princess instead of hacking off her head."

Peter sighed dramatically and reached out his hand. "Okay, sport. Hand over the sword. Mama says no more fencing."

Isaac began to wail and didn't stop until I'd popped a video into the VCR. The child development experts can shake their heads all they want. TV is an essential tool of the modern parent. How else can two adults have a conversation during the day? I'm all for stimulating my children's tiny little developing brains, but sometimes you just need them to sit in one place and be quiet. My kids are going to have to be couch potatoes when I have something I absolutely must do. Like tell their father that I'd stumbled across yet another suspicious death.

"He killed himself?" Peter asked.

"I guess so. I mean, it looks that way with the gun and everything, but it seems so unlikely. He was such an upbeat kind of guy."

"Aren't methamphetamine addicts sort of by definition upbeat? It's called speed for a reason."

"He wasn't an addict. I mean, he was, but he wasn't using anymore. He'd been in recovery forever."

"How can you be so sure?"

"What? That he wasn't using?"

"It's not like he'd necessarily admit it to you if he *was* using. And you did always talk about how hyper he was."

"Hyper in a *good* way. Like a trainer is supposed to be. Not like some whacked-out speed freak. I think I'd know the difference," I said. I certainly should know the difference. In my career as a federal public defender, I'd spent plenty of time with people addicted to all different sorts of substances. I'd had heroin-addict clients to whom I'd needed to give at least twenty-four hours' notice that I was planning to drop by the Metropolitan Detention Center if I didn't want them to be completely stoned when I had them brought down to the visiting room. As a young lawyer, it had taken me a while to figure out that they were wasted, not because they weren't acting high, but just because I was so naive that it never occurred to me that the federal jail would be such an easy place to score. It turns out you can get pretty much anything at the MDC, and the prices aren't much more than out on the street. Don't ask me how they get the drugs into the jail. I suppose a cynical person might suggest taking a look at the fine display of automotive splendor in the prison guards' parking lot.

I'd represented my share of methamphetamine dealers, mostly Mexican guys who brought the precursor chemicals in over the border and cooked them up in labs out in the wilds of Riverside, or aging bikers who kept themselves in Harley parts doing the same. I knew a speed freak when I saw one, and by the time I met Bobby Katz, he wasn't using. I was sure of it.

"He wasn't using," I said firmly.

"Okay. Well, maybe he just did a good job of hiding how depressed he was. Maybe that whole thing with his girlfriend was harder on him than you thought. Maybe *she's* using again, and he couldn't stand it anymore."

"Maybe," I said doubtfully. "But isn't it a bit more likely that he'd just leave her?"

Peter shrugged. "When is the funeral?"

"I don't know. I guess that depends on when they release the body. If they decide it's a suicide, I'm sure it will be soon. Bobby's Jewish, and that means his parents will want to bury him as soon as possible."

Three

"WHY is it that wearing black to a funeral seems ostentatious?" I said to my pint-sized companion. "I mean, you're supposed to wear black. That's the traditional color of mourning. Unless you're Buddhist. Not that white would be any easier. I mean, I own literally nothing white except panties and bras."

"Wear this, Mommy. It's black," Ruby said, pulling my one full-length gown out of its dry cleaner bag.

"I don't know, honey. Sequins on a Sunday morning?"

Ruby nodded. "They're *black* sequins."

"Let's try something less formal, shall we?" I waded to the back of my closet where I'd consigned my business attire. I pulled out a charcoal pantsuit and brushed the dust off the shoulders. I pulled on the slacks, exhaling while I zipped. "Ruby, hand me one of your hair elastics, would you?"

She pulled one out of her ponytail, and I picked the clump of red hair out of it. I hooked one end around the button at the waistband of the pants and the other through the buttonhole. With that extra couple of inches, I could get away with the pants. Just. I found a pale gray cotton knit sweater and shrugged on the suit jacket.

"So? What do you think?" I asked my four-year-old daughter.

"Gorgeous. But a little fat."

I gave her the stink eye and pinched her on the tush. "Go tell your daddy I'm leaving."

The L.A. county coroner had released Bobby's body a week after he died. Jewish law requires that a body be buried as soon as possible after death, within a day or two, so his parents arranged for him to be buried the day following the body's release. Sometimes *halacha* has to give way to the exigencies of the criminal justice system, but all things considered, I thought the county had done a pretty good job of finishing their work expeditiously. It probably helped that they didn't need to worry about what the body looked like; we're not allowed to have open caskets, so no one besides the undertaker was going to see whatever remained of poor Bobby Katz.

The turnout for Bobby's service was impressive, considering that it took place all the way out in Thousand Oaks. I got there early enough to take a strategic place in the back and watch people as they came in. Bobby's friends from work were sitting in the first few rows. I noticed that none of them had had my doubts. To a one they were impeccably turned out in absolute, unremitting, pure black. The women wore severe dresses and suits that were just a shade too tight, and the men all seemed to have bought the same Armani funereal attire. I thought the midnight ties were a bit over-kill, but then I had an elastic band around my waist, so who was I to comment?

Behind them were a couple of rows of what had to be friends from Alcoholics and Narcotics Anonymous. They were a diverse bunch: old and young, nicely dressed and decidedly sloppy. It took a moment for me to realize that Betsy sat among them. I could just see the back of her bent neck leaning against the shoulder of an overweight woman whose thick gray ponytail was tied with a piece of red yarn. I considered getting up and paying my respects but decided to wait until after the ceremony. Older couples—most likely friends of Bobby's parents—took up the rest of the seats. I couldn't see anyone who looked like his family.

After a few more minutes, a door opened, and Bobby's family filed in. They sat down in a few rows of chairs set up to the side of the hall, and one of the ushers drew a large wooden screen in front of them, effectively shielding them from view. Odd, I thought, but then I hadn't been to that many funerals.

The service was quick; the rabbi spoke briefly about lives cut short before their time. A man who identified himself as Bobby's brother described their bucolic life as children. He told us about Bobby's earlier high school drama successes and his struggles in Hollywood. Bobby's brother said how proud he and the rest of the family had been when his younger sibling had ultimately found professional satisfaction. Except that he described Bobby as a physical *therapist,* not a trainer. I suppose Bobby might have gone to school and been certified as a physical therapist, but somehow I didn't think that was something he'd keep a secret from his clientele. He'd certainly never mentioned that to me.

After Bobby's brother sat down, a beefy man in an ill-fitting blue blazer rose to his feet and looked as though he might begin to speak. He was sitting with the AA crowd, and they all raised their faces to him expectantly. He opened his mouth but then caught sight of the rabbi. The rabbi shook his head vigorously and frowned. The man blushed and, appropriately chastened, sat back down. The rabbi launched into a final prayer, and then it was all over. The usher rolled back the screen, and Bobby's family walked back out of the room. I caught a glimpse of his dark-haired mother, her face drawn and gaunt. Her narrow, colorless lips were pinched in a thin line, and she leaned heavily on the arm of a younger woman with similar coloring, whom I imagined must have been Bobby's sister. As soon as they'd gone, I squeezed past the exiting guests in the direction of Betsy and her friends.

"Hi, Betsy," I said.

"Oh, Juliet," she wailed and fell out of her friend's arms and into mine. "Did you see that? They wouldn't even let me *sit* with them. The funeral director wouldn't let me into the *room* with them. He said, 'Family only,' and threw me out."

I patted her back and murmured a few comforting words.

"It's disgraceful, is what it is," said the gray-haired woman.

"Betsy's the *widow* for crying out loud." The other friends and supporters who'd gathered around us murmured in agreement.

"Did you talk to Bobby's parents, Betsy?" I asked.

She nodded, her face pressed against my shoulder. Then she sniffed and picked up her head. "Oh, sorry," she mumbled. "I got your jacket all wet."

"Don't worry about it. I have two kids, remember? I'm used to having snot on my clothes."

She smiled wanly.

"Have you spoken to his family?" I asked again.

"Yeah," she said. "His brother came by a couple of days ago to tell me that they were going to *let* me stay in the apartment until the end of the month. Like they have a right. It's my home. They can't throw me out."

This was worse than I thought. "And his parents?"

"They won't even talk to me. I finally got through to them, and his dad said that their *lawyer* told them not to talk to me. Can you believe that? I mean, Bobby and I were *engaged*. We had a date and *everything*. The *rabbi* is talking to me. Why can't they?"

"What did the rabbi say?"

"He came by the same day as Bobby's brother. He said he wanted to see how I was doing, but who knows why he was really there. She probably sent him to make sure I hadn't stolen the TV set or something."

"She?"

"Bobby's mother. God, I hate her."

The gray-haired woman put her hand on my arm. "We're

having a potluck after the burial. Since none of Bobby's AA family is welcome at his parents' home, we're hosting our own reception at Betsy's house. You're welcome to join us."

"Thanks," I said. I followed the group out of the hall and down a long, winding path of crushed white rock to the burial site. I stood with the AA contingent on the outskirts of the crowd and watched as the members of Bobby's family gathered around the grave. The coffin was perched on a hydraulic lift over the gaping hole. There was a pile of earth covered in a large piece of what looked like AstroTurf to one side of the open grave, and the air was redolent with the meaty smell of soil and grass. The rabbi began to sing the prayers in his deep, atonal voice, and a few of the onlookers joined him. Dredging up the Hebrew words from somewhere deep in my memory, I murmured along with them. The deeply familiar prayers brought tears to my eyes, yet I found them soothing and peaceful. So slowly that it seemed almost imperceptible, the coffin began to sink into the grave. It landed with a faint and final thump, and, one by one, each member of Bobby's family took a small trowel full of dirt and spilled it onto the coffin. After the last of them had gone, Betsy pushed forward and took the trowel out of the pile of earth. She dumped the dirt into the grave and cried, "I love you, Bobby. We'll be together someday. I promise you."

I glanced over at Bobby's parents in time to catch his mother's face pinch into an angry scowl. Bobby's father reached an arm around his wife and drew her away from the scene. The two of them, flanked by their children, walked back to the waiting limousines.

• • •

SINCE the ban on the presence of recovering addicts at Bobby's parents' home after the service obviously did not include me, I decided to head over there with the rest of the guests. I got the address from Laurence, Bobby's boss, and found my way to a large Mediterranean-style home set far back from the road on a block of almost identical houses. Bobby's parents had put out quite a spread, and it was a little while before I could pry myself away from the buffet table. Finally, having gorged myself to a rather embarrassing degree on blintzes, whitefish salad, and those fruit minitarts that are ubiquitous at every L.A. event, be it a funeral or a movie opening, I made my way through the crowd in the direction of Bobby's family.

They were making a fairly symbolic effort at sitting shivah, the traditional Jewish mourning ritual. They sat on low chairs, but they all wore their shoes and had on little black polyester scarves that they'd torn at the corner, instead of rending their own garments. I know that's not unusual, that only the ultra-Orthodox still tear their clothing, but still, it seemed somehow to belie the sincerity of their mourning, like they were sad, but not sad enough to ruin a good shirt. I stood in a line of people and finally reached Bobby's mother.

"I'm so sorry for your loss," I said, echoing everyone else. What else is there to say?

"Thank you," she murmured and looked beyond me at the next person.

"Um, I was a client of Bobby's," I said, trying to keep her attention.

"Oh?"

"He was a wonderful trainer. So knowledgable."

She didn't answer, just nodded politely and reached out her hand to the woman standing behind me.

"I'm so sorry for your loss," the other woman said.

I wandered through the line, expressing my condolences to the rest of the family. His two sisters and brother all looked quite a bit older than he'd been, the oldest sister by as much as a dozen years. But then, Bobby might have been older than I thought. His business did require a certain youthful appearance.

I stood for a while in a corner of the room and then caught the eye of a short man with a hairline that had receded to the purely hypothetical. He sidled over to me.

"Were you a friend of Bobby's?" he asked.

"A client. And a friend. I'm Juliet Applebaum," I replied.

"I'm Larry. He was my brother-in-law. I'm married to Michelle."

"Bobby's sister?"

"The younger one. Over there, that's Lisa, she's the oldest. And that's her husband Mitch." He pointed to the dark-haired woman seated next to Bobby's mother and to a tall, stooped man with an oversized nose sitting on the couch and leafing through a magazine.

"Did he just have the one brother?"

"Yeah, David. Dot com David."

"Excuse me?"

"Didn't you know? David is Cyberjet. The Internet portal? He's worth like a hundred million dollars, even after the crash."

"Wow," I said, delighted to have found someone at once close to the family and indiscreet.

"Wasn't Bobby getting married?" I said. "Where's his fiancée?"

Larry snorted. "Betsy? No way Arthur and Leslie would ever let her into the house. She's a drug fiend. And, anyway, *I'm* betting she had something to do with Bobby's death."

"Really?" I asked. "I thought it was suicide."

"Who's to say she didn't drive him to it? Anyway, the cops haven't ruled out murder."

That explained their insistence on getting a statement from Betsy. "Do the police consider the fiancée a suspect?"

"Probably. At the very least, she drove him to it. That's what Arthur and Leslie think, anyway. Like I said, she's a drug fiend."

"Didn't Bobby and Betsy meet in recovery?"

He snorted. "I wouldn't mention that around here if I were you. We're not allowed to talk about Bobby's little problem. The most Arthur and Leslie will admit is that he had a period of 'youthful indiscretion.' "

At that moment, Larry's wife joined us. She, like her mother, was slim and dark-haired. Her mascara was smudged and her nose tinged with red. She looped her arm through her husband's and smiled at me wanly.

"I'm Juliet. I was a client of Bobby's," I said.

"Thanks so much for coming. It really means a lot to my

parents, to all of us, that so many of Bobby's colleagues and clients came today," she said.

"He was a lovely guy," I told her, feeling my eyes fill.

"He was. He really was." The tears flowed freely down her cheeks. "He's always had just the biggest heart. He was the kind of kid who brought home stray cats and lost dogs."

Larry shook his head. "Gee, your mom must have just loved that."

Michelle smiled through her tears. "Oh, she went ballistic. He'd hide them in his room until one of the cleaning ladies would find them and tell my mother. Once he hid a rat in his closet for like a month. And not a white rat, either. A big gray street rat. Then, one day while he was at school and Lisa was home from college, she was digging around his room for something or other, and she opened up this plastic shoe box with holes punched in the top. She started screaming and ended up kicking the box over and the thing got loose. My mother had the exterminators in within an hour, and there was rat poison all over our house for days. They never caught the rat, though. He's probably still living in the basement."

We made small talk for a while longer, during the course of which Michelle told me what Bobby had already told me months before: Their parents were both doctors. Their father was a surgeon and their mother a pathologist on the faculty at UCLA. The girls had followed in their footsteps. Lisa, the older sister, and her husband Mitch had an obstetrical practice in the Valley. Michelle, a research scientist with both an M.D. and a Ph.D., was a statistical geneticist with Biogenet, a biotech company that specialized in creating disease-resistant seed.

"Wow," I said. "A doctor, a scientist, and an Internet entrepreneur. It can't have been easy competing with you guys."

"No," she admitted, "but then Bobby didn't really try to compete. He wasn't academically inclined. From the time he was a little kid, he said he was going to be an actor. That's all he really wanted. He didn't even go to college."

"That must have been something of a disappointment for your parents."

"I guess so, but then they never really expected that much from him. I mean, not academically. He wasn't like the rest of us. He just didn't have that kind of brain."

She sighed and leaned against her husband. "I should go sit next to Mom. Are you okay on your own, Larry?"

"I'm fine. Juliet's keeping me company. Aren't you?" he said with a leer.

Michelle didn't seem to notice her husband's wolfish expression. She nodded distractedly and left us.

"Intense family dynamic," I said to Larry.

"You don't know the half of it," he whispered.

"Really?" I leaned closer to him and raised my eyebrows.

He was obviously flattered at the attention and altogether too happy to be dishing his in-laws to an encouraging ear.

"It can't hurt to talk about this now. I mean, the poor guy's dead. Arthur and Leslie never expected much from Bobby because they're big believers in the heritability of intelligence."

"Excuse me?"

"They expected their kids to be brilliant because they think they are such perfect genetic specimens. But not Bobby."

"Why not?"

"Because Bobby wasn't theirs. He was adopted."

"Really?" This shocked me. Bobby and I had had long talks about our families. He'd never mentioned this.

"You want to know the really messed up thing?"

I nodded.

He glanced over his shoulder and motioned me closer. I leaned in, and he said in a low voice, "They never told him."

"Really?" I matched his whisper. "That's so strange. Why not?"

"They said it was because they didn't want him to feel inferior. But David, Lisa, and Michelle all knew. Michelle's the baby, and she was eight when they brought him home, so of course they knew. The whole family kept it a secret from Bobby."

"He *never* knew?"

"No. I mean, he didn't know until recently."

"And how did this suddenly come out?"

"Totally by accident. It had something to do with his being a Tay-Sachs carrier. David knows. He's the one who told him."

BECAUSE it was some time before I could corner Bobby's brother David, I had to satisfy myself instead with reinvestigating the buffet table. I was strategically placed to take advantage of the tray of tiny pecan tarts that made their late appearance on the arm of a white-jacketed server. I was wolfing down my third when I saw David start to walk out of the living room. I wiped my mouth and slipped out after him. I found him slumped in a cracked leather armchair in a library, away from the noise of the crowd. I smiled at him as I entered the room, then gazed admiringly at the walls of books.

"What a beautiful room," I said.

"Yeah. My parents keep all their medical texts in here. When Bobby was little, I used to get the dermatology ones down and scare him with pictures of pustules and varicella and the like."

"Gross."

"He loved it. He'd squeal and shriek and then say, 'Show me another one.' We really liked the V.D. pictures."

I lowered myself into the matching armchair opposite Bobby's brother. "You gave a lovely eulogy."

"I guess. I didn't really know what to say. I mean, what do you say when your kid brother dies?"

The question was rhetorical.

"Were you two very close?"

"No. I mean, we got along, but, you know, I was twelve when Bobby was born. I left for college when he was six. I didn't come home much after that."

"Still, it sounds like you loved him very much."

David shrugged and wiped tears from his eyes with an angry fist. "Yeah," he croaked.

"I'm Juliet, I was a friend of Bobby's. And a client."

He shook my hand perfunctorily.

I didn't really know how to ask David what it was that I wanted to know, but it's always served me well just to open my big mouth, so that's what I did. "I hope you don't think I'm prying, but I was wondering, well, what you make of Bobby's death. I know it's not really any of my business, but Bobby didn't seem at all depressed to me, and I saw him pretty regularly. Do you have any idea why he would have killed himself?"

David looked at me for a moment, as if surprised at my audacity. Then he said, "No. Honestly, I don't. I mean, I thought for a while it might have been because . . . well, because of something that happened, but then he didn't seem depressed at all to me, either, even after everything, and I just didn't think it could be . . . that."

"You mean Bobby finding out that he was adopted?"

"You know about that? He told you about that?" David sounded surprised.

I nodded, figuring I was answering the first question, not the second.

"I thought it might be that at first," David said. "But you know, I don't really think it could be. I mean, he freaked out when I told him, but he was mostly pissed off at Mom and Dad for keeping it a secret. He didn't seem depressed about it. On the contrary."

"On the contrary?" I asked.

"Well, you know Bobby. He never really felt like he fit in this family. He always felt like an intellectual failure around here. He seemed almost relieved to find out that he wasn't biologically related to the rest of us. He even said to me something like, 'So I'm not a freak of nature; I'm just a regular person.' " David sounded as if he were trying to convince himself rather than me.

"He found out because of the Tay-Sachs diagnosis?" I asked.

"Yeah. I guess you know that I told him."

I nodded.

"The rabbi made him do genetic testing before the wedding. Bobby called me after he got the results of his Tay-Sachs screen. He came to me because he knew that Lisa and Michelle would have had to be tested when they got married. But I'm not married. He wanted to tell me that he was a carrier and that I might be, too. I told him I wasn't worried about it, but he, you know, pressed me. So then I finally told him. I mean, why not? I never thought it *should* be a secret. I never agreed with Mom and Dad that we should pretend he was just like the rest of us. I mean, he had a *right* to know. Didn't he?" He held his hands out beseechingly. I wanted to make him feel better, to reassure him that he'd done the right thing. I had a feeling that, his protestations notwithstanding, David was terrified that he'd done something awful by telling his brother about the adoption. Deep inside, he was probably desperately afraid that what he'd said had driven Bobby to suicide.

"I certainly think he had a right to know," I said. "How did your parents react to his finding out?"

David grunted in disgust. "They were furious with me.

My dad still isn't speaking to me. My mother just gave me one of her trademark 'I'm so disappointed in you' speeches. Neither of them was really willing to talk about it with Bobby. They confirmed it, and that was that. We weren't supposed to speak about it ever again."

"And did you speak about it again? Did Bobby?"

He heaved a sigh and ran his fingers through his hair. "He tried, I think. But you have to understand, once my parents decide to dig their heels in, that's pretty much it. I know Bobby was hoping to get information about his birth family out of them, but it's like getting blood from a stone."

Poor Bobby. I could imagine him trying to find out about himself, eager for any scrap of information. "Do you know if Bobby ever did learn anything about his birth family?"

At that moment, David seemed to decide he'd confided enough in a stranger. He just shook his head and got up out of his chair.

"I should be getting back." He opened the door to the library and waited for me to follow him.

Four

I wanted to make an appearance at Betsy's gathering. It was the decent thing to do, and it would give me the opportunity to find out more about Bobby's adoption. Finding out that fact about himself had surely resulted in a considerable amount of personal turmoil. Perhaps it had even been enough to lead him to kill himself.

I called Peter from the car to let him know I'd be out for longer than I'd expected.

"There's someone here who has something to say to you," he said.

Then I heard a high-pitched squeak. "Mama?"

"Hi, Isaac. How are you doing, buddy?"

"I want to nurse. Come home right now, and bring me my breasts."

Peter got back on the line.

"I suppose you think that's funny," I said.

"He's been bugging me all day. When are you going to wean this kid?"

"I'm *trying*. You know I'm trying." And I was. I'd been trying to wean Isaac since he was eighteen months old and announced, in a loud voice in the middle of a restaurant, "This side empty. Other side, please." But the kid clearly had other plans, and they included breast-feeding his way through college. Whenever I tried to hand him a bottle, he would fling it across the room and dive-bomb my shirt front. Nine times out of ten, I would give in, if only to quiet the shrieking. Peter thought I was way too much of a softy, but he'd never experienced the humiliation of sitting on an airplane next to a toddler screaming, "Give me my breast *now!*" at the top of his lungs.

While the quality of the food at Betsy's wasn't quite up to that of the Drs. Katz, the ebullience of the crowd made up for the hodgepodge of a buffet. The room was packed with people weeping, laughing, and sharing reminiscences of Bobby. I greeted a few of those I'd met at the funeral and made my way over to Betsy, who was sitting on the living room couch, smiling through tears at a story told by a muscular man with a shaved head.

"And then I was like, 'I'll go first,' and Bobby was like, 'Okay.' And then as soon as I start screaming, he decides, no he doesn't want to get his tongue pierced, he's never going to get his tongue pierced, and goddamn it if he didn't check himself into rehab two days later. When I got sober, we started telling people that it was fear of this," the man stuck out his tongue, revealing a large silver stud, "that got Bobby on the wagon."

The small crowd of people huddled around Betsy and the bald man groaned and laughed. I slipped in between them and put a hand on her shoulder.

"Hey," I said. "How are you holding up?"

She shrugged. "Okay, I guess. I'm just glad Annie arranged for all this. I couldn't have dealt with being on my own after that horrible funeral."

"I went to the Katzes," I said. "I found out a few things that I'd like to talk to you about."

"What's going on?"

I looked around at the crowd of interested faces. "Is there somewhere we could go to talk?"

Betsy led me down the hall to the bedroom. She flopped on the bed, and I sat on the edge of a sling back chair, doing my best not to fall through the torn seat.

I told her briefly about my conversation with David. Betsy started to shake her head.

"What are you talking about?" she asked, her brow wrinkled and her eyebrows raised in shock. "Adopted? Bobby was adopted?"

"Didn't he tell you?" That floored me. Bobby hadn't told his fiancée about what was surely one of the greatest surprises of his life?

Betsy shook her head. "I can't believe this. I mean, I'm really surprised. Not that he's adopted. I'm just surprised he didn't tell me. I thought we told each other everything."

"You're *not* surprised that he was adopted?"

She shook her head. "It makes sense; I mean, how could *that* woman have given birth to a wonderful, sweet, generous guy like Bobby?" She sniffed.

"Were you guys doing okay?" I chose my words carefully. "I know you'd had some difficult times lately."

"You mean when I got busted, right?"

I nodded my head.

"Yeah, well, Bobby really helped me through all that. He stood by me and even went along with the wedding plans, in spite of everything. In spite of his parents trying to convince him to dump me."

"And you don't have any idea why Bobby might have committed suicide?"

She shook her head. "No. And, honestly, it doesn't make sense to me. Not a bit. It's just not something that Bobby would do. He's not that kind of person. I mean, I was supposed to be the pessimist in our relationship." She barked a hoarse, sad laugh and then started crying again.

At that moment, I realized that I wasn't going to be able to just walk away from Bobby's death. Call it compassion, call it an inability to leave well enough alone, call it plain old-fashioned nosiness. I couldn't live with myself without at least trying to find out why Bobby Katz had died and who, if anyone, was responsible.

I sat down next to Betsy and took her hand. "Would you be willing to let me look into things a bit, maybe do a little investigation? I've got some experience with this kind of thing. Maybe I can help figure out what happened to Bobby."

She looked at me curiously and said, "I don't mind. I mean, it's not like the police are doing anything, as far as I can tell." Her face brightened momentarily, and it seemed to me that she liked the idea of having an ally, of having at least one other person in her corner, trying to figure out what had happened to the man in her life.

"Would you mind if I look through some of Bobby's things? His papers or his computer? It could give me an idea of what was going on with him, maybe lead me in the direction of whatever was bothering him or even whoever might have wanted to hurt him," I said.

"I guess that would be okay. The cops took a lot of stuff, but they left his laptop. Do you want to see that?"

"That could be useful."

Bobby had turned their second bedroom into a small home office. He had a computer table set up against one wall and a four-drawer filing cabinet in the corner. I shut the door of the room against the sound of Bobby's friends, who had begun singing versions of his favorite songs—he must have been a big Billy Joel fan—and started rifling through the filing cabinet. The cops had pretty well cleaned it out. I could see where he had a folder with each of his clients' names printed across the top, but the contents of the individual files were missing. I found my own and couldn't resist checking, but it, too, was empty. They'd left the drawers full of articles on weight control and fitness innovations pretty well alone, but I didn't think those would be particularly useful to me. I was impressed with how carefully Bobby organized his information files, though. He was a man who took his work seriously and clearly tried to keep up in the field.

I turned my attention to the computer, hoping that the cops hadn't wiped the hard drive. Luckily, they'd either ignored it or perhaps had made a copy of it for themselves. I felt vaguely guilty searching through Bobby's files. A person's computer is as intimate as his underwear drawer, and it reflects his character even more. Bobby's hard drive was as tidy and orderly as he was. He had carefully organized his files; his folders were all divided into subfolders. In a folder named "Work," I found a client list with phone numbers and addresses that I printed out on the inkjet printer cabled to the laptop. I clicked my way through his various folders, hoping I might find a diary of some kind. No luck. I was about to open a folder temptingly called "Correspondence" when my purse started ringing.

"*Oy,* Peter, I totally lost track of time. Is everything okay?"

"It's fine," my husband said, "but the kids are asking for you. I'm about to start dinner, and I need to know if you plan to make it home."

"Oh God, is it that late?"

I promised I'd be home right away and went to find Betsy. Most of her friends had gone home, and she sat in the living room with the last few. When I walked in, she looked up from the photo album she'd been leafing through.

"Did you find anything?" she asked listlessly.

"Not really. Not yet. Listen, Betsy, would you have any objection to my borrowing Bobby's computer? I'd copy the hard drive here, but I'm afraid it would take me hours to get everything."

She shrugged her shoulders. "Go ahead and take it. I don't care. If his brother comes around, I'll tell him you have it. Otherwise, he'll probably think I pawned it or something."

Five

OVER breakfast the next morning, I decided that if I was going to investigate Bobby's death, I would need some expert advice. I don't know what I'd do without Al Hockey. Never in my life would I have imagined that I could rely so unreservedly on someone who collected semiautomatic weapons for pleasure. Al and I are about as divergent politically as two people can be, but in some strange way that neither of us understands, we're friends. Al is an ex-cop who retired from the force after taking a couple of ounces of lead in the belly. He'd been working as a defense investigator at the federal public defender for a few years when I got hired, and we hit it off almost instantly. He'd investigated all my cases for me and had saved me from many an embarrassing mistake. He's been a terrific source of information, both legal and less-than, ever since.

"What do you want?" he growled when I called him. "I'm packing."

"Packing? What do you mean packing? Are you moving?"

"No. Quitting. Today's my last day at the office. You're lucky you found me here."

That came as a shock to me. Al's retirement from the LAPD had lasted all of six months before he'd taken the public defender job.

"You're not retiring?" I asked him.

"Please. I'm going to go freelance."

"Freelance investigation?"

"Yeah. A couple of weeks ago at the Dodger's game, I bumped into Vinnie Hernandez, a guy I knew from the LAPD. Turns out he retired two years ago. Now he's making six figures."

"Freelancing?"

"Exactly."

I poured a sippy cup of orange juice and handed it to Isaac, who had his legs and arms wrapped around my leg.

"Like a private eye?" I asked.

"Vinnie's billing out at a hundred bucks an hour, working for private criminal defense attorneys. The guy's a complete idiot, and in twenty hours a week, he's making twice what I do in forty."

"So you decided to quit."

"You bet. I'm no fool. I'm sick of baby-sitting public defenders. I'm going to hang out a shingle, print up some business cards, and start living large."

I mopped up the sippy cup's worth of orange juice that

Isaac had just expertly spilled all over the floor and opened a cupboard full of pots and pans.

"Does that mean that now I have to pay you a hundred bucks to get you to make a call for me?" I said.

"That depends, Juliet of the black leather miniskirt." Was he never going to let me live down my youthful indiscretions? Why oh why had I ever thought that skirt was an appropriate thing to show up in on my first day of work?

Isaac went to work on the pots and pans, drowning out Al's next question.

I put a finger to my ear and shouted, "What?"

"Do you want to go into business with me?" Al replied, also shouting.

At that moment, Isaac grabbed a wooden spoon and smacked me with it on the shin, as hard as he could. I grabbed his fat little hand and wrenched the wooden spoon out of it. "No!" I yelled.

"That's pretty definite," Al said.

"What? No. I mean, I don't know. Wow. What an offer. You're really asking me to become a PI?"

I could swear I heard him roll his eyes. "I'm not talking *The Rockford Files* here. I plan on doing your basic criminal investigation. Skip tracers. Maybe some death penalty work. That kind of thing."

"Wow," I said again, not particularly articulately.

"Don't answer me now. We'll get together sometime soon and talk about it. What did you call me for?"

I filled him in on Bobby's death.

"What is *with* you, Juliet?"

"Excuse me?"

"You're like some kind of human Ebola virus or something. How many dead people do you trip over in the course of a week?"

"Funny. Ha ha. So, will you call up your friends at the LAPD and find out what's going on with the investigation? Mostly, I want to know if they're considering it a murder or a suicide."

"Yeah, I'll make some calls. Give me a day or two, okay?"

"Great. Thanks, Al."

After I hung up the phone, I scooped Isaac up, disengaged him from the drum kit he'd made out of the set of Magnalite cookware I'd gotten from my mother as a wedding present, and went in search of his older sister. I found her in her bedroom, carefully pasting bits of colored paper, yarn, and other scraps to a large sheet of poster board.

"Get him out of here!" she shrieked, draping her body over her art.

"Oh Ruby, don't be so melodramatic. He's not going to do anything."

The words had barely left my mouth when Isaac grabbed a plastic bottle of Elmer's glue and squeezed a huge white puddle out on the carpet.

"Oh my God! No, Isaac! No!" I shouted.

"You see! You see! He ruins everything!" Ruby echoed my yell. I mopped up the spill, yanked her squirming brother out the door, and shut it firmly behind me.

"Well, clearly you're not going to be playing with Ruby this afternoon," I said. "Look, kid, I need to do some work on the computer. Your daddy's going to be home from his meeting in about an hour. Can you think of something to do by yourself until he gets home?"

"TV?" my angelic child suggested with a bat of his eyelashes.

"Right. Fine. As a special treat."

He ran to the couch and scrambled up. I sorted through our bedraggled video collection until I found a copy of *Color Me Barbra*, a Barbra Streisand TV special from some time in the 1960s. Ruby loved it because she was obsessed with show tunes. Isaac liked it because La Streisand does half the numbers inside of a tiger cage. With real tigers.

I set Bobby's laptop up next to my computer and connected it to our home network with an Ethernet cable. Now I could freely copy documents and files from it onto my own hard drive. I went back into his correspondence folder and spent the next half-hour skimming through letters to clients and friends until I found something. I had a feeling about it even before I opened it, because the document wasn't titled like the other letters in the folder, with the recipient's name and the date. It was just called "Letter #1."

The letter started out somewhat cryptically. Underneath Bobby's standard letterhead—an old-time circus strongman holding up his address—the salutation read simply, "Hello."

I don't even know how to address this letter. Dear Mom seems wrong; I already have a mom, and you probably wouldn't want me to call you that. Calling you by your name seems so formal. So, maybe I'll just leave it blank. I guess you've probably figured out who this letter is from. My name is Bobby Katz, and I'm your birth son. I was born on February 15, 1972. I was placed for adoption on that very day through Jewish Family Services.

I've had a pretty happy life. My adoptive family gave me the best of everything, and any problems I have had were my fault, not theirs. I didn't even know I was adopted until I had some genetic testing done in preparation for my wedding (I'm getting married in six months to a wonderful girl named Betsy). Once I found out about myself, I registered with the State of California Reunion Registry. I was hoping that you might have done so, too, and was pretty disappointed to find that you hadn't. I understand, though, that it's pretty common for birth parents not to be registered—most people don't even know the registry exists!

I won't tell you how I found you—I don't think it would be fair to the people who helped me. But I did find you. And I'm hoping you'll be willing to write or E-mail me or maybe even to meet me.

The letter went on to describe Bobby's job and interests, and he closed with another plea to his birth mother to write or E-mail him.

I leaned back in my chair, touched by the hope with which Bobby had sent this letter to someone who, for all he knew, had no interest in establishing any kind of contact with him whatsoever. How must it have felt to find out, as an adult, that you weren't who you thought you were? Or, at the very least, that some of the basic tenets of your life and sense of self were lies? Had Bobby's mother refused his attempts at contact? Had he responded to that rejection with despair? Had he even *sent* the letter? Why wasn't there an address?

My reverie was interrupted by my growing consciousness of a suspicious sound: silence. My house was never silent, except when my children were either asleep or engaged in some act of nursery terrorism. I hustled out to the family room, where I found Isaac sitting, slack-jawed and glassy-eyed, staring at Barbra's flaring nostrils and purple boa. I tiptoed away. I put my ear to Ruby's door. She was singing softly to herself; the tune seemed to be her own version of "Bohemian Rhapsody," which her father had for some reason considered it not merely appropriate but desirable to teach her.

It was a miracle. My children were actually giving me a period of uninterrupted peace.

I went back to my desk and sat for a minute, tapping my finger against the keys. The police had confiscated the contents of Bobby's filing cabinet, so there was no way for me to see if he'd ever gotten a reply from his birth mother. However, I could check to see if he'd gotten an E-mail. I'd already noticed that Bobby kept careful track of his paper files and the documents on his computer. It stood to reason that he would do the same with his E-mail records.

He didn't disappoint me. His E-mail program had a carefully organized archiving system. Unfortunately, because I didn't know his mother's name or E-mail address, it was going to be a challenge sifting through the hundreds of messages in the "Personal Correspondence" archive to find which one might have come from her. Using the program's Find command, I started searching by E-mail subject heading. "Birth Mother" came up with nothing, as did "Mother." "Mom," however, led me to a series of E-mails from Bobby's sister, Michelle, complaining about how their mother had criticized Michelle's new living room furniture. Apparently, Michelle had bought it at IKEA, and Dr. Katz felt constrained to point out that in Sweden, where the chain had begun, and which the good doctor had recently visited to deliver a paper on "Fluorescent In Situ Hybridization," IKEA was considered about as classy as Wal-Mart. Michelle had written to Bobby seeking reassurance 1. That IKEA was a reasonable place to buy a couch, and 2. That their mother was a bitch. I searched through Bobby's "Sent Mail" file and found that he had responded to both in the affirmative.

Subject headings "Adoption," "Adopt," and "Adopted" led nowhere. Finally, I decided I had to find a more efficient way to search. I launched Bobby's Internet browser and looked up his favorite sites. The California Reunion Registry was listed, but I already knew that Bobby hadn't found his mother through that site. Nothing else in the favorite sites list looked promising, so I clicked down the Go button, hoping he had given his browser a large cache. He had. The browser allowed me to track the last two hundred web sites he'd visited immediately before he died.

Bobby had searched a medical site for a cure for athlete's foot (I made a mental note not to shower at the gym) and bought a Palm Pilot on-line. He'd posted a review of the

new John Grisham on Amazon.com (he liked it okay but
wasn't thrilled) and bid on a set of golf clubs on eBay. None
of these activities, I thought, was that of a man about to kill
himself. As of a day or two before his death, Bobby had
planned to be around long enough to monitor a five-day on-
line auction and receive a package that would take three to
seven days to arrive. If he *had* committed suicide, it had
been a spur-of-the-moment decision. I wondered if the police
had come across this information.

Bobby had also, I noticed, checked his I-Groups home
page over and over again. I-Groups is one of the many sites
on the web that allows people with similar interests to join
up in E-mail circles. The site has hundreds of different
groups, some open to the public, some open only to those
approved by the members of the group. Being part of an E-
mail circle through a service like I-Groups lets members send
messages to the group as a whole, instead of having to cc
each individual member. I was part of a couple of these
circles myself. Friends from college and I had been E-mailing
for quite some time. When I was pregnant with Ruby, I'd
joined a list for mothers due in the same month and spent
a very self-indulgent and satisfying nine months comparing
stretch marks and hemorrhoids. For a while, I'd participated
in an I-Group for "recovering attorneys" but found the "support" I got a bit over the top. I mean, it wasn't like I'd
weaned myself off heroin; all I'd done was quit my job.

I held my breath as I selected the I-Groups link in
Bobby's Go menu. If he hadn't saved his password as a cookie
to be entered automatically when the page came up, there

would be no way for me to check his I-Groups home page and access the archives of posted messages.

I was lucky. Like me, Bobby was not particularly security conscious. His home page showed just one I-Group. It was called Parentfinder@I-Groups.com. I clicked over to the archive and began sifting through the messages. Bobby had joined the group almost three months before. His initial message informed the other members that he was an adoptee looking for his birth parents, who were not registered with the California Reunion Registry. He asked for advice about alternative ways to find them. And boy did he get it.

As I scrolled down through the many replies to Bobby's initial posting, I was interrupted by the scourge of the work-at-home parent: her children. Ruby and Isaac wandered into the room. Isaac was naked from the waist down.

"Isaac! Where are your pants?" We'd only recently convinced Isaac to lose his diapers. It had taken about forty pounds of M&M's doled out one by one as a reward for each successful bathroom excursion.

"They're in the toilet," Ruby said as if I were an idiot for even asking.

"Oh, no. Did you go to the bathroom, Isaac?" He nodded happily, sucking on the two middle fingers of his left hand. I stifled my gag reflex and hustled him back to the bathroom. I fished his pants out of the toilet and briefly considered throwing them directly in the trash. They were from Baby Gap, however, and not even a toilet full of poop justified tossing out a thirty-dollar pair of toddler jeans. Instead, I dumped them into the washing machine. As I scrubbed my disgusting yet adorable boy from tush to fingertip, I wondered, not for the first time, if I'd still be wiping the kid's behind when he was in graduate school. Probably not. Probably by the time he had his bar mitzvah, he'd be able to handle his own potty needs.

I'd clearly ignored the kids for long enough. I gazed longingly at the TV, but guilt won out over my desire to keep reading Bobby's E-mail. Instead, I spilled a load of blocks and miniature cars on the carpet. I groaned softly as I sat down. I know there are some mothers who love nothing more than spending hours finger painting and making Play-Doh castles. I'm not one of them. Don't get me wrong, I adore my kids. I love them with a combination of ferocity and obsession that can be overwhelming both to them and to me. But playing with them can be skull-crushingly tedious.

Ruby and I played with the blocks while Isaac zoomed his Hot Wheels around us. I did my best to convince her not to bellow in protest when he dared approach our construction site. I was less successful at getting him to stop talking about how his cars were going to shoot and kill each other. We compromised by agreeing that the red Formula One could beat up the other cars, as long as he gave their booboos kisses afterward.

After half an hour or so, my garage built out of blocks was teetering dangerously, and I wasn't sure if I had the energy to rebuild. Luckily, Peter showed up just as I was beginning to lose focus. As soon as he'd gotten down on his hands and knees and begun renovating my structurally unsound building, I slipped back to my computer.

Within an hour, I'd made a long list of potential means of finding a birth parent who didn't want to be found. Bobby's E-mail pals had provided him with names and numbers of private investigators, on-line search services, and a few organizations dedicated to furthering an individual's access to his or her biological and familial history. According to his E-mails to the group, Bobby had contacted the organizations first, so that's what I did. I checked out their web sites. By and large, they seemed fairly innocuous, mostly providing the same kind of support that Bobby had gotten from his I-Group.

One was a little more intense. This site, called www.right toknow.net, was dedicated to assisting people whose birth parents were not just unknown but were actively keeping their identities secret. The site offered more arcane investigative services, including instructions on performing skip traces and credit card searches. It offered the names of investigators who specialized in "fugitive parents." At the bottom of the home page was an E-mail address. I copied it and then clicked over to Bobby's E-mail program. I searched his archives for any message from that address. Pay dirt.

Over the past couple of months, Bobby had been E-mailing with someone named Louise, the founder of Right to Know. From her E-mails, I pieced together that Bobby had contacted her through the web site and asked for help with finding his birth mother. Early on in their correspondence, she told him that she, too, lived in Los Angeles, and that she had sources for finding parents in the area. Louise sent Bobby E-mails almost daily. I read through a pile of them before I found one that sounded promising. In it, Louise told Bobby that she had "good news" and "information." She asked him to meet her where she worked, at the Starbucks across the street from the Westside Pavilion, a mall in West L.A.

I copied all the important information onto my computer. It had taken me all of an afternoon to get within one step of Bobby's birth parents. The Internet seems to have been designed to allow people to spy on one another. It certainly has made the private detective's job significantly easier. I found this somewhat troubling, although I was less concerned with the death of privacy than with the possibility that Al would find a significant portion of his new business usurped by a web site's offering to find anything about anybody at bargain basement rates.

six

THE next morning, after I'd dropped Ruby off at preschool, Isaac and I headed out to the Westside Pavilion. I guess it probably says something about my approach to detective work that before I went to question Louise, I did a little shopping. I had never actually bought new clothes for Isaac. He'd spent the first two and a half years of his life wearing Ruby's hand-me-downs. Suddenly, however, as if in concert with his burgeoning interest in firearms, he'd begun to refuse to allow me to dress him in her old pink overalls, flowered T-shirts, and pastel leggings, although for some reason he was still perfectly happy to sleep in her Little Mermaid nightgown.

Isaac and I stocked up on navy blue shirts, royal blue pants, and indigo sweatshirts from the sale racks in the various baby stores. I hung my purchases over the handle of his stroller, and we rolled out of the mall onto Pico Boulevard at the corner of Westwood Boulevard. There, directly across Pico from us, was a Starbucks. Across Westwood, and at the other end of the block, was another Starbucks. Now, granted, Westwood is a busy street, and they were at either end of a fairly long block, but still—was there really enough latte business for two identical coffeehouses?

"Shall we flip a coin, buddy?" I asked Isaac.

He looked up at me quizzically. "Okay," he said.

"Heads we go to the one down the block, tails we go to the one on the other side of the street."

It came up tails. Isaac was fascinated. "Do it again," he said.

"Okay." It came up heads.

"Third one breaks the tie, buddy." Tails.

I waited for a pause in the traffic and then, shopping bags flapping in our wake, jaywalked as fast as I could across the street. Isaac shrieked delightedly at both the speed of our run and the fact that we were very clearly breaking the "cross at the corner" rule I'd so carefully drilled into his head.

I walked up to the counter and ordered a tall, fat, skinny, wide something or other and asked the pierced young thing behind the bar if Louise worked at the store. A dark-haired woman with bad skin, who was studying the foaming action she was getting from her steam-valve machine, lifted her head at the sound of my voice. I smiled at her, sure that I'd found my Louise.

The boy with the studded eyebrow to whom I'd asked my question said, "No, I don't know any Louise."

"Are you sure? I know there's a Louise working either here or at the Starbucks down the block. Is your manager around? Maybe I could ask him or her?"

The boy shrugged his shoulders and jerked his head toward the woman. The thick ring in his nose jiggled with the action, and he reached up a hand to steady it. God help me if my children decide to have themselves pierced. Peter swears that the fad will be over by the time Ruby is a teenager, but I am convinced that will only be because they will have come up with something worse, like voluntary amputation, or recreational trepanning.

The dark-haired woman came over to me, her face blank. Her cheeks were pitted and scarred, and a few angry pimples covered her chin and nestled in the corners of her mouth. "I'm the supervisor. Can I help you?"

"I'm looking for someone named Louise. Does she work here?"

"We don't have anybody by that name," she said.

"Oh. Well, maybe it's the Starbucks at the end of the block. I'll try there."

"Don't forget your latte," the pierced boy called. I went back for the cup and balanced it on the handle of the stroller as I tried to open the door. I couldn't manage to hold the coffee, open the door, and push the stroller through at the same time, and neither employee seemed particularly interested in helping me. Finally, I tossed the latte in the trash and, holding the door open with one hand, pushed Isaac and his stroller out with the other. I'd get a coffee at the next Starbucks.

Isaac and I reenacted our dangerous and illegal asphalt traverse and headed to café number two. The next Starbucks was a slightly larger version of the first, with a few extra tasteful banquettes and little round tables. This time, the person with the nose ring who took my order was female. She shook her head immediately at my question about Louise and handed me my extra-foamy mocha with a smile that seemed much too sweet for her severe haircut and jewelry. I pulled Isaac out of his stroller, handed him a madeleine, and fed him the foam from my coffee.

I turned to ask the coffee girl if she was sure that there was no Louise when Isaac's bellow of rage made me spin around in my chair.

"What happened?" I asked, checking him over for broken bones.

"My cookie!" he wailed.

"What about your cookie?"

"It got in your coffee!"

"How did it get in my coffee?"

"I tried to scoop the foam, but it melted my cookie!"

I tried to comfort him, but finally just got him another cookie. His face broke into a grin to rival that of the Cheshire Cat. It had been an elaborate ploy to weasel another madeleine out of me.

"Okay, cookie boy, let's go."

We wandered back down the street toward the mall and our car. As we got closer to the other Starbucks, I kept thinking of the supervisor with the bad skin. I was sure that when I'd first said the name Louise, she'd raised her head in recognition. I mentally kicked myself in the pants for being so dense. A pseudonym. It was entirely possible that the name Louise was merely an alias. Given the fact that some of the "suggestions" on the web site seemed a bit on the gray side of legality, it was reasonable that "Louise" might not want to be directly associated with it. She would want to avoid liability, not to mention the wrath of parents whose identities she'd given away over their objections.

Once more I hauled Isaac back across the street. I walked into the store and up to the front of the counter, without waiting in line.

"Hey! There's a line here, you know," a voice snarled at me. I ignored the muscle-bound man in the shiny suit who'd yelled at me and caught the dark-haired woman's eye.

"Hi," I said. "I'd like to talk to you."

She flushed and shook her head. "Sorry, we're busy."

"I'll wait," I said and leaned against the counter. Isaac started kicking the glass pastry case. Helpful child.

She glared at me and then, finally, shrugged her shoulders and motioned for another young employee to step into her spot at the register. She ducked out from behind the counter and led me to a table in the far corner of the café.

I pulled a few board books out of the basket of the stroller and settled Isaac on a bench not too far from where the woman had sat down. Between the books and the sugar packets on the table, he was set for a few minutes at least.

"Hi, Candace," I said, reading the name tag pinned to her chest.

She didn't answer.

"I think we have a friend in common."

"Yeah? Who?" She sounded like she didn't think it was very likely.

"Bobby Katz."

Her face flushed again, and she looked down at her fingernails. They were bitten red and raw.

"You know Bobby?" she murmured, the harshness gone from her voice.

I realized at that moment that she hadn't heard. I dreaded being the one to tell her. I reached out my hand and grasped hers.

"I'm so sorry to have to tell you this," I began.

She jerked her hand out of mine. "What?" Her voice was a hollow croak.

"Bobby died ten days ago. I'm so sorry."

Her skin seemed to gray before my eyes. The acne and scars stood out crimson against the ashen pallor. "What? How?"

I took a breath before launching into the ugly details. I also lowered my voice so that Isaac wouldn't hear. "It's not real clear. What we know for now is that he was found dead in his car along the PCH, just south of Santa Monica Canyon. He was holding a gun, and it looks like it was probably a suicide."

"No!" The people standing in line for coffee looked our way at the explosive sound of her voice.

Isaac whined softly, "Mama?"

"It's okay, honey," I said. I walked over and gave him a hug. He was making neat stacks of sugar, Equal and Sweet'N

Low, alternating the white, blue, and pink packets. "You keep playing, okay?"

He nodded, and I went back to Candace. Her face was buried in her hands, and she was worrying the pimples on her forehead with her fingers.

"I couldn't figure out why he hasn't been answering my E-mail. I've been writing like ten times a day for over a week," she said.

I realized then that I'd been so busy reviewing his archives that I hadn't thought of checking Bobby's E-mail account for *new* messages that had come in since his death. I made a mental note to log on from his laptop once I got home and download all his pending messages.

"Candace, I'm hoping you can give me some information."

She looked at me suspiciously.

"I'm doing a little checking around for Betsy, Bobby's fiancée. We're trying to figure out what was going on with Bobby in the last couple of months of his life."

At the sound of Betsy's name, Candace's jaw tightened.

"I can't help you."

"I think you can. I know Bobby found you through Right to Know's web site. I know you were helping Bobby find his birth parents. Can you tell me a little more about your organization?"

She leveled a suspicious gaze in my direction. "Like what?"

"Well, for example, you're an organization for adoptees looking for their birth parents, right?"

"Not only. We have some birth parents, too. Anybody

who's looking for information. But, yeah, it's mostly lost children."

The term surprised me.

"What kind of information do you provide?"

"RTK is really a clearinghouse, more than anything else. We pool information, get ideas on where and how to look. That kind of thing."

"And you started it?"

"I got the idea after I spent two years tracking down my birth mother. I ended up finding my family through the Lost Bird Society. They help lost and stolen Indian children find their way home. I'm Lakota. Part. My birth mother is half-Indian. Her mom lived on the rez her whole life."

Now that I looked closely, I thought I could see a trace of American Indian; maybe it was just the dark hair, or the not-quite-prominent cheekbones.

"Did you find your birth mother?"

Candace shrugged her shoulders. "Yeah, but she didn't want to have anything to do with me. She'd really been co-opted by the dominant culture, you know? But my grandmother, her mother, she was great. I got to know her pretty well before she died. Meeting her was like coming home. If I hadn't been stolen from my people, I might have grown up on the reservation, instead of in Newport Beach."

I resisted the urge to point out that to many people, it might be preferable to grow up in an exclusive beach community rather than a pre-casino-era Indian reservation rife with unemployment and substandard schools and health care. But, then, what did I know about the spiritual vacuum experienced by American Indian children growing up away from their tribes?

"You founded Right to Know to help others in your situation?" I asked.

"Yeah. The thing is, nobody really cares about the kid in all this. Everybody is so worried about the rights of the birth mother and about the adoptive family. But nobody considers that the kid has a right to know who she is, even if her birth mother is trying to hide from her."

"Why?"

"Why what?"

"Why does a child have a right to know? If the birth mother gave her up and doesn't want to be contacted, why should the child be told who the mother is?"

Candace glared at me, furious that I'd questioned her orthodoxy.

"Well, the most obvious reason is medical. I mean, look at Bobby. If he hadn't gotten tested, he might have ended up having a baby with that horrible genetic disease, what's it called?"

"Tay-Sachs."

"Yeah, Tay-Sachs. He's lucky; he got tested. But what if he hadn't?"

"Well, his fiancée would have had to have been a carrier, too. But I understand what you're saying. There are lots of genetic diseases that people should have information about."

"You can't imagine what it's like to go get a physical. The doctor starts asking you for all this information about family history, like cancer or diabetes. And you have nothing to say except 'I don't know.' It's terrible," Candace said, banging on the table to punctuate her words. "Why should adopted kids be deprived of medical history information that could save their lives?"

The intensity of her emotions surprised me, and I inadvertently drew back from her. She noticed my reaction and blushed.

I didn't want to make her uncomfortable, so I said in my most reassuring voice, "That's a good point. I've never really thought of that. But couldn't we solve that problem by requiring birth parents to provide medical histories when they relinquish their babies?"

She pushed herself back in her chair and shook her head vigorously. "You don't get it. It's not just the medical stuff. It's about your identity. I'm an Indian. You know what that means? That's the reason I never felt at home in the white man's world." She waved angrily around her at the benches, the carefully selected prints and posters, the little wooden tables, the white coffee drinkers. "My whole life I felt like I didn't belong. And if my birth mother had had her way, I'd have never known why. Well, now I know. I'm a Lakota woman. And nobody can keep that from me. Not even my mother."

She banged her fist on the table, again, hard. Isaac looked up, frightened, and I motioned him over with my hand. He ran up to me and I scooped him into my lap.

"Thank you so much, Candace," I said. "I hadn't thought of these issues before, and I appreciate your taking the time to educate me." We both knew I was buttering her up, but

I smiled my sweetest smile anyway. "Betsy, Bobby's fiancée, is desperate to figure out what was happening with him. I understand that you found out something important for Bobby, and that he met you here at the store. I need you to tell me what it was that you told him."

"Why should I tell you? I don't know you. I don't even know Betsy." The name sounded like curdled milk on her tongue.

"Please, Candace. I'm not trying to get you in any trouble. I'm just trying to track Bobby's actions for the period before his death. We need to find out why he killed himself. *If* he killed himself."

She looked at me with narrowed eyes. "Do you think someone murdered him?"

Did I? That seemed even less likely than that the cheerful, optimistic man had committed suicide. "I don't know. That's one of the things I'm trying to find out."

"What are you, some kind of a detective?"

I paused at that. How much easier it would have been to say, "Yes, right. A detective." Instead, I shook my head. "I'm just a friend. Candace, please. What did you find out?"

"How do I know you're not trying to pin all this on me?" she said, crossing her arms over her shelflike chest.

That brought me up short. Pin what on her? Bobby's death? I shook my head. "I'm not trying to pin anything on anybody. I'm just trying to find out if Bobby ever found his birth parents. And I know you can help me."

"Mama," Isaac whimpered. The tone of our conversation was obviously frightening him. I couldn't continue this in front of him. I wrapped him in my arms and gave him a kiss. Then I dug around in my bag for one of the business cards Peter had made up for me the previous Christmas. They were a pale moss green with my name, telephone numbers, and E-mail address engraved in a darker shade of the same color.

"Here's my number. Call me if you decide you're willing to talk. In the meantime, you'll forgive me if I turn your name over to the detectives investigating Bobby's—" I looked down at Isaac in my lap and bit off the last word of my sentence.

"No!" Candace said. Then, seemingly embarrassed at her own vehemence, she continued, "I'd prefer not to be involved. For the sake of Right to Know."

She paused for a moment and then, leaning forward, whispered, "All I can tell you is that Bobby was born at Haverford Memorial Hospital in Pasadena. That's all I know. But it should be enough for you to find his mother."

seven

AL'S new office turned out to be a phone line, a card table, and a dented filing cabinet shoved into one corner of his garage in Westminster, a small city just south of downtown L.A.

"Nice digs," I said.

I'd called him on my way home from meeting Candace to ask his advice on how to find the names of all the babies born at Haverford Memorial Hospital on February 15, 1972. I'd also asked him what he'd heard from his friends on the force.

"It looks like a suicide," he had said.

"But they're not sure?"

"There are some ambiguities."

"Like what? Explain to me what they look for when

they're evaluating a suspicious death to determine if it's suicide or murder."

"A variety of things. The presence or absence of a weapon."

"And they found a gun in the car."

"In his hand, actually."

"Right, in his hand. What else?"

"They look at the trajectory of the bullet. You know, could a person have shot himself at that particular angle."

"Did they do that in Bobby's case?"

"Yup, but it didn't get them very far. The trajectory is consistent with suicide, but that obviously doesn't rule out murder."

"Anything else?"

"Sure. The presence or absence of fingerprints in the car."

"And?"

"And there were fingerprints. Lots of them. Your friend had a lot of passengers."

I sighed. "Anything conclusive? What about residue on his fingertips? If he had fired the gun himself, wouldn't there be gunshot residue?"

"You're getting good at this, girl. Sure, there would."

"And was there?"

"Some."

"Some?"

"Some. Not as much as you might expect, but enough to be consistent with suicide."

"Basically, what you're telling me is that there's not enough conclusive evidence either way."

"Right now, the forensic evidence could lead to either conclusion: suicide or death by person or persons unknown."

"Well, where does that leave the cops? What do they do next?"

"That depends. There was no note, so they could treat the death as a murder, investigate the family, that kind of thing."

"And will they?"

"Maybe. It depends how many other murders the detectives have on their plates."

I told Al about Bobby's on-line purchases. "Why would someone contemplating suicide buy a Palm Pilot?" I asked. "It doesn't make sense."

"You're right. It does seem unlikely. But maybe it was a spur-of-the-moment kind of thing. I'll tell you what I'll do. I'll call my friend and suggest that someone check into Bobby's credit card bills in the days before his death. They've probably already done it, but it's worth a word."

"Thanks, Al."

"No problem. I'll let you know what I find out about the hospital, too."

Al called two days after our telephone conversation and invited me over for a "consultation." I'd left Isaac with Peter—they had big plans to check out the new titles at Golden Apple Comics—dropped Ruby off at preschool, and headed down to Westminster.

I sat down in a white vinyl chair Al brought out from the kitchen for me.

"So, how's business?" I asked.

"Getting there. Listen, have you given any more thought to my idea?"

"You mean about joining you in this flourishing endeavor?" I asked, waving my hand around the garage.

"Hey, this is only temporary. Pretty soon I'll be able to afford office space, but until then, the wife said if I'm going to be home all day, the least I can do is get out from under her feet."

"I don't know, Al. It looks like a one-man operation to me."

"This is just the beginning. Like I told you, I'm going to start doing defense investigation, maybe some death penalty work. I could really use someone like you—someone whose legal experience would complement my investigative skills. It would be worth your while, Juliet. At a hundred and fifty bucks an hour, the money's going to be rolling in."

I nodded, not wanting to rib him anymore when he clearly had such faith in me. "Why would my legal experience be useful to you? I don't know much of anything about investigation. That's why I'm always bugging *you* for information."

He leaned back in his chair and propped his feet up on the card table. He was wearing pale blue Sansabelt slacks with a slight flare, a gold shirt, and navy socks with white clocks. His shoes seemed to have been made out of the same material as my chair. I wondered if they came as a set.

"Because you're a defense attorney. You know how to put together a case. You know what kinds of things to investigate, what's relevant, what's not."

"But the lawyers you're working with will tell you what they want investigated. They'll put together their own cases."

"True. But having that added expertise would give us an edge on the competition. And how many times have I heard you say that two-thirds of the criminal defense lawyers out there don't know their asses from their elbows? Just because they're paying us doesn't mean they have any idea what we should be doing."

That made sense to me. "But I'm not licensed."

"You don't have to be. That's the beauty of it. I'm a licensed private investigator. You work for me. We call you a defense specialist, or a mitigation specialist if we're doing a death case, and then you don't need to take the investigator's test or do the obligatory hours. Or, if you want to, you can apply for your license, take the test, and then do your hours with me."

The idea did have a certain appeal. Since I'd quit work, I'd found myself increasingly bored and frustrated with staying home. I'd left my job because I thought raising my kids myself was more important than working, but sometimes it was difficult to imagine that my sighing, listless presence around the house was really doing Ruby and Isaac any good. The only time I'd been really happy over the last couple of years was when I'd been doing what amounted to investigative work. Only then did I feel like I was taking advantage of my skills and my intelligence. At the same time, however, I wasn't ready to give up and go back to work even if pushing a stroller might not have been doing it for me.

"The whole point of quitting the defender's office was that I wanted to be home with my kids. If I wanted to go back to work, I'd go back to being a lawyer."

"Aren't your kids in school by now?" Al asked.

"Ruby's in preschool. But Isaac's just a baby. Almost. He's two and a half."

"He'll be in school soon, too. What are you going to do with yourself while the kids aren't home? Are you planning on going back to the defender's office then?

He'd hit the nail on the head. What was I going to do when Isaac started school next year? Going back to a public defender's rigorous schedule didn't appeal to me. Someone had to pick the kids up every day after school, and Peter's schedule was just too unpredictable. If I went back to my job, I wasn't going to be able to be there when the kids came home. I'd show up in time for dinner, like I'd done when Ruby was a baby. I hadn't wanted to do that then, and it wasn't looking any better to me now. On the other hand, I wasn't one of those people who could while away the school day at aerobics classes or volunteering at the local hospital. I was going to have to find something else to keep my mornings busy.

The idea was sounding better all the time. But was I really ready? I didn't think so. "I don't know, Al. I'll think about it. Anyway, are you going to charge me a hundred and fifty bucks an hour to tell me how to find the mothers who gave birth at Haverford Memorial on February 15, 1972?"

Al smiled. "Nope. You're still on the discount plan."

"Thanks. So, how do I go about tracking down the mothers?"

"You read this list." He swung his feet off the table and pushed a sheet of paper across to me. On it were the names of seven women.

"What's this?"

"The mothers who gave birth at Haverford Memorial Hospital on February 15, 1972."

"No way! How'd you get this?"

He smiled mysteriously. "Secret of the trade, I fear. Available only to other investigators."

"C'mon, Al!"

"Come work for me and find out."

I kicked his ankle, hard.

"Okay, here's what I did. It wasn't that difficult. The hospital keeps records of births, obviously. Nowadays, those records are all computerized, and if you're allowed access, or if you can somehow get into the system, the records are there at a touch of a button. However, because of patient confidentiality, it's a challenge, to say the least, to get into the system. We were lucky, though, and Haverford Memorial never bothered to computerize its old records. I figured right off the records probably wouldn't be stored at the hospital—they take up too much space. I called a few of the larger document storage facilities and found the one the hospital uses to store its old records. It wasn't too far from here, so I just took a little drive on over."

"And they let you in to look at the documents?"

"Well, let's just say that a well-placed gratuity did the trick. You owe me a hundred bucks."

I got out my checkbook and wrote him a check, which he pocketed with a gracious "Thank you."

"No, thank *you*," I said.

"Lucky for us the records were very well-organized. I found the births recorded by day and date."

Together we went over the list. Four of the women who had given birth to babies on Bobby's birthday had had girls. The mother of one of the three boys was named Michiko Tanazaki. I figured I could safely rule her out. That left two women, a Brenda Fessler who in 1972 was nineteen years old and a Susan Masters, who was twenty-six.

Al promised to run a skip trace on the two and happily accepted the check I wrote him to cover the costs of the search. Then the two of us went inside to say hello to his wife.

Jeanelle Hockey was a lovely, dark-skinned woman with perfectly ironed hair who favored twin sets and knee-length skirts. In many ways, she seemed an unlikely mate for Al, who, with his golf clothes and military haircut, was the last man you'd imagine in an interracial marriage. The two had met in the late 1960s, when he was a uniformed police officer, and she a civilian employee of the Los Angeles Police Department. They'd been married almost thirty years and had three daughters in their twenties.

When we walked in from the garage, Jeanelle was going over Al's gun collection with a pink feather duster. I'd only been to Al's house a few times, and the sight of the racks of shotguns and cases of handguns and vintage pistols still made my skin crawl. He could tell I was nonplussed, perhaps because of the grimace on my face and the loud retching noises I made.

"Want to hold one?" he asked, deadpan.

"No! What is it with boys and guns? Isaac's as obsessed with them as you are. Why? Can you explain this to me? Is it a phallic thing?"

Jeanelle smiled and said, "If it's phallic, then I don't know what that says about me. I've been a target shooter for years. And our youngest, Robyn, is nationally ranked in the biathlon. She was an alternate for the Olympic team."

"Wow," I said. "What's that? Shooting and biking?"

"Shooting and skiing," Al said. "Robyn's an incredible athlete. She's at Cal State Northridge now, but she's thinking about Quantico."

"The FBI?"

"Yup. She'd make a great cop."

Jeanelle handed me a large photograph of a beautiful, carefully made up young woman aiming a rifle. Her curly brown hair was held off her face with a tortoiseshell clip, and her nails were long and painted a brilliant shade of aquamarine.

Al's daughters were all gorgeous and successful. And unmarried. A glance at the artillery around the room made it all too obvious why. Their father probably blasted a hole in any guy who dared show up at the front door.

WHEN I got home from Al's, I found my house empty and the light flashing on the answering machine. The first message was from Peter, telling me that he and Isaac would pick Ruby up from school and then go to the zoo at Griffith Park.

I heaved a sigh of relief at having been spared the trip to that grim place with its tiny cages and palpable air of animal desperation.

The rest of the messages were from Betsy. She'd left four, and by the last one she was hysterical. By replaying her messages a few times, I managed to figure out that David Katz had come by for Bobby's things and had been upset to find the computer missing. I tried to call her and had the eerie shock of getting Bobby's voice, asking me to leave a message at the tone. He sounded absolutely like himself, down to the trademark instruction to "make the most of" my day. The hair on the back of my neck stood up. For a moment, I was surprised that Betsy had left his voice on the machine, but then I considered what I would have done under the same circumstances. I didn't think I could have borne to erase Peter's voice, either.

I debated leaving a message but decided to go to the apartment instead. Betsy had sounded so distraught that it wouldn't have surprised me if she were immobilized in bed.

She was anything but. I found her standing in the middle of her living room with the apartment door wide open. She was swigging water from a bottle and pacing frantically back and forth.

"Betsy?" I said.

"Oh God! Thank God it's you. Tell me you have the laptop. Do you have it? Did you bring the laptop? Is it with you?" Her words tumbled out of her mouth in an agitated rush.

"I have it." I held up the computer.

"Oh, thank God. I was really freaking out. You have no idea. I mean, that creep was over here basically screaming at me—telling me that if I didn't come up with the laptop he was going to, like, sue me or something. I hate that whole family. Honestly I do. You have no idea. I hate them."

I looked closely at Betsy. She took a mouthful of water and then brushed her hair away with an angry jerk of her hand.

"What are you on, Betsy?" I kept my voice soft and neutral.

She snapped her head in my direction. Her lower lip trembled. "What are you talking about? What are you accusing me of? You're just like them. You're all the same."

I walked over and put my arm around her, and to my surprise, she let me lead her to the couch. She sat down, her leg twitching, and then her face crumpled. She sagged into me and began to cry.

"I'm sorry. God, I'm so sorry. I didn't mean to do this. I just . . . I just couldn't help myself. I was so freaked out by Bobby's brother. I mean, he really scared me. I called you!" She glared at me accusingly.

"I'm sorry. I was out."

"Yeah, well I called you. And I called my goddamn sponsor. Everybody was out. I mean, what am I supposed to do? My boyfriend is dead, goddamn it. I mean, if that didn't make me fall off the wagon I wouldn't be *human*."

"What did you take?"

"Nothing. A couple of pills. Like barely anything. Just to feel a little better. A little hopeful. I mean, what's wrong with that? Do you know how long it's been since I felt good? I'm not even asking for good, goddamn it. Just the, like, absence of pain would be nice for a minute."

I was disgusted with Betsy, despite myself. I know addiction is a disease—one that's difficult and often impossible to cure. Bobby had done it, however, and so had she, at least for a while. It seemed an utter betrayal of his memory and the faith he'd had in her for her to be using. "Maybe it's time to try your sponsor again," I suggested.

She whirled around. "Are you *nuts*? Are you totally insane? What am I going to say? 'Hi Annie, I'm wired out of my mind. Wanna come over and play?' "

"No, but you can ask for help. Do you want to go back on the meth?"

She stuck her chin out defiantly.

"Do you want this to be the end of your sobriety? Do you want to go to jail? You're still on probation. If your drug test comes up positive, they're going to take you out of the diversion program and send you right back to court. If that happens, you and I both know that there is a very good chance you'll have to serve some time."

Her lip trembled again. "I don't want to go to jail." She began crying in earnest and pointed to a corner table. I walked over and found Annie's pager number taped to the wall above the telephone. I dialed the number and hung up the phone. It rang almost immediately.

THE gray-haired, matronly woman from the funeral was in the living room within half an hour. She held Betsy in her arms while the young woman wept. I sat watching them for a moment and then took the laptop back into Bobby's office. I hooked up the modem and launched his E-mail program and web browser. I went to Yahoo.com and set up an E-mail account with a pseudonym for myself. It didn't hurt to be cautious. I downloaded all his new messages to his laptop and then forwarded the contents of his in box to my new Yahoo E-mail address. Now I had the messages, and I was the only person who knew I had them.

I found Betsy and Annie still huddled together on the couch.

"This has to get to Bobby's parents," I said, lifting the laptop that I'd zipped into its case.

Annie nodded.

"I don't think she's in any shape to take it over," I said.

"No, I don't think she is."

"Should I do it?" I asked.

Annie nodded, and Betsy just cried harder.

Eight

BOBBY'S brother David answered the door of the Katzes' house. It took a moment for him to remember me from the funeral. He invited me in somewhat warily and directed me to the large living room where the shivah had taken place. His mother was sitting on a sleek brown couch, her legs tucked up under her and her spectator pumps carefully lined up on the carpet, under the coffee table. She looked up from the medical journal she was reading and made a halfhearted attempt to rise. Motioning for her not to bother, I sat down in a tweed armchair opposite the couch. The room was entirely furnished in shades of brown and taupe. The carpet was discreetly patterned in various browns, the furniture was all soft earth shades. Even the paintings on the walls were mud-colored. A large, dark landscape of a dry hillside hung over the fireplace, and a series of small oblong prints in tones ranging from a rich cream to an almost black brown hung along the wall over the couch. Dr. Katz herself was dressed in an off-white cashmere turtleneck and a brown wool skirt. She matched her décor perfectly.

"Hello?" she said, doubt in her tone, obviously wondering what I was doing there.

"I'm Juliet Applebaum, a friend and client of Bobby's. I met you at the funeral, although you probably don't remember me."

"Yes, yes, of course." She arched an eyebrow expectantly.

"What can we do for you, Juliet?" David asked.

I lifted the computer bag off the floor an inch or two. "I'm returning Bobby's computer for Betsy. She asked me to bring it to you; I understand you came by their apartment looking for it."

David flushed a bit, as though he were for the first time considering what an outsider might think of his stripping Bobby's fiancée's home of all of its valuables.

"We, um, we just wanted to make sure that Bobby's things were taken care of. Given Betsy's . . . problem."

I handed him the computer. I wasn't going to tell him that I understood his actions, although in a way I guess I did. Betsy's relapse might or might not have had to do with David's visit. I could certainly understand how Bobby's family would be angry with her and suspicious of the role her drug use might have had in his death. On the other hand, given how much money these people obviously had, did they really need to be prying knickknacks and small appliances out of Betsy's hands? What difference would it make to them if she kept the computer—or sold it to buy methamphetamine for that matter?

"Why didn't she just give me the computer when I was there picking up Bobby's other stuff?" David asked.

"Because I had it," I said, wondering exactly how I was going to explain why.

The two looked at me quizzically. I thought of lying for a moment, telling them that I'd borrowed the computer before Bobby's death, but like I tell Ruby whenever I catch her stretching the truth, there's really nothing quite as embarrassing as when a lie comes back and bites you in the butt.

"I asked Betsy if I could look through Bobby's files."

"Excuse me?" Dr. Katz's voice was sharp. "You were going through my son's computer files?"

"What the hell is this about?" David asked, leaning forward in his chair.

"Betsy and I were hoping that there might be something in Bobby's computer files that would give us an idea of why he killed himself. Or if," I added, trying to sort of slip it in.

Dr. Katz's eyes narrowed. "If?"

I nodded. "It's my understanding that the police have not made a final determination as to suicide or . . . or murder."

Bobby's mother closed her eyes for a moment. "Forgive me, Ms. . . . Ms. . . ." she murmured.

"Applebaum."

"Ms. Applebaum, I'm afraid I still don't understand why you were going through Bobby's personal belongings, or why you imagined that you had the permission to do so."

This time it was my turn to blush. "Betsy gave me permission. As Bobby's fiancée and the cohabitant of his apartment, I felt she had the right to do so." My language was getting as stiff and formal as hers.

"Are you some kind of investigator?" David interjected.

If I had just taken Al up on his offer, I could have simply said "Yes," and that would have been that. "No, but I'm an attorney, and I specialize in criminal law. I've done some . . . some freelance investigation in the past. Informally. I'm doing the same for Betsy."

"What exactly is it that you are doing? And why did you need Bobby's computer?" Bobby's mother asked.

The two looked at me, Dr. Katz's face stern and haughty, her son's heavy with grief and confusion.

"I read through some of Bobby's E-mail, trying to discover whether his search for his birth parents might have something to do with his death."

Dr. Katz's face tightened.

"You should have told him, Mom," David muttered.

She glared at her son. "This is not the time, David," she snapped. Then she turned to me. "And," she said, "did it, in your opinion?"

"Excuse me?" I said.

"Did Bobby's misguided search for his 'birth mother' "— she wrinkled her nose as she said the words—"have anything to do with his death? In your opinion?"

"I don't know yet," I said. "Did Bobby talk to you about his birth mother? Did he tell you whether or not he had found her?" I didn't tell the Katzes that I had all but tracked her down by myself. First I wanted to find out what they knew.

"I was not interested in discussing the issue with my son. Nor am I interested in discussing it now, with you. Bobby told me that he was looking for this woman. I discouraged him. I told him that as she had not been concerned with his welfare when he was an infant, it was unlikely that she'd want any contact with him almost thirty years later. I also told him that neither I nor his father would participate in any further discussion of this adoption nonsense."

"Oh for God's sake, Mom," David said.

She turned on him. "What? For God's sake what? This is your fault, David. Had you just had the decency, the *intelligence,* to keep your mouth shut, none of this would have happened. Before you took upon yourself the role of truthsayer, Bobby was perfectly happy, as were we all."

"Right. Perfectly happy. He was a drug addict, Mother. A drug addict."

"Addiction is a disease. A disease, what's more, with a strong genetic component."

David jumped out of his seat. "Sure, Mom. None of this is your fault. Bobby took crank because he's genetically inferior. Not because of anything you did. It has nothing to do with the fact that you made him feel like a failure his entire life. It has nothing to do with the fact that you never even bothered to expect him to succeed. No, that's not why the poor schmuck got high. It has nothing to do with *you.*"

He pounded out of the room and through the front door, slamming it behind him.

Dr. Katz sat still in her chair for a few moments. Then she turned to me. "I apologize for my son's behavior."

I didn't say anything. I didn't know what to say.

"David is upset. He feels responsible for Bobby's death. He knows he should never have told Bobby about the adoption."

"Why did you keep it a secret, Dr. Katz?"

She paused, as if considering whether to answer. After a moment she said, "We saw no reason to tell him. Bobby was our son. Our feelings for him were in no way different than our feelings for our other children. Highlighting for him the difference would only have hurt him. And hurt him it did. All of this has only served to prove to me that I made the right decision."

"If you don't mind my asking, why did you adopt Bobby?"

"I don't mind," she said, sounding surprised at her own willingness to discuss this with me. "My husband and I had always planned to have four children. But, after my third Caesarean section, my obstetrician discouraged me from undergoing the procedure again. He claimed it was dangerous. I understand now from my daughter that this was unnecessarily conservative advice. Had we known that, Arthur and I would have gone on to have another child of our own."

The regret in her voice was unmistakable.

I didn't know how to respond to this, and she seemed immediately to regret having so clearly indicated how she felt about being forced to adopt when she would rather have given birth to her own baby. We sat silently for a moment.

I fidgeted a bit with my feet, crossing and uncrossing my ankles. She sat perfectly still, the only visible motion in her body the slight flare of her nostrils as she inhaled.

Finally, she said, "If there's nothing else I can do for you . . ." Her voice trailed off.

I rose quickly to my feet. "Would you like me to keep you apprised of what I discover?" I asked.

"So you intend to continue to . . . to investigate?" She sounded as though the very word made her skin crawl.

I nodded. "I'm sorry."

She shook her head slightly and then, rising to her feet, led me to the front door.

Nine

THAT evening, Peter announced that he wanted to have a celebratory dinner but refused to tell me what we were celebrating. The four of us went to Giovanni's, an Italian restaurant located in a strip mall not too far from our house. Giovanni's is our favorite restaurant, and we've been regulars for years. Despite the unprepossessing surroundings, the food is fabulous—simple and delicious.

The kids went straight back to the kitchen, where they knew the chef and his mother were sure to slip them some before-dinner *panna cotta* or almond nougat. Peter and I took our usual table and ordered our usual bottle of Chianti.

"What are we celebrating?" I asked, raising my glass.

"Two things. First of all, Parnassus agreed to Tyler's counteroffer. I'm going to do *The Impaler*. And they're already talking about a twenty- or thirty-million-dollar budget."

"Wow! That's fabulous. And they caved on your quote?" Hollywood screenwriters spend their lives trying to raise their "quotes," the amount they are paid per picture.

"Not by as much as Tyler asked, but by enough. Definitely enough. We're a little closer to buying that house."

"Peter! I'm so proud of you." I was dying to get our family out of the duplex apartment where Peter and I had been living since we moved to L.A. Every time we put aside enough money for the down payment on a house, however, real estate prices shot a little higher. By now they were stratospheric, and I was beginning to lose hope. This was very good news.

"Yup, I'll be bringing home some bacon now," my husband said.

"You're amazing. Really." I kissed him on the cheek. "Without you, we'd be in the gutter." Without him, I would probably have stayed at my fancy law firm and be raking in the high six figures by now. But I wouldn't have been happy. Not for a minute.

"So what's going on with this thing with your trainer?"

I brought Peter up to date on what I'd found out. I described the complicated situation with Bobby's adoption and how I had narrowed down the list of possible birth mothers to two. I also told him about Candace and her crusade.

"Pretty intense," Peter said.

"No kidding."

"You know, sometimes I wonder. If you have kids, and you adopt another, is it really possible to love the adopted kid as much?"

"I suppose it must be. For some people. I don't think the Drs. Katz succeeded very well, though."

"It must be hard. I mean, think about how much time we spend talking about how much Ruby looks like you, or about how Isaac has my ability to focus on an issue."

"Focus? I think *obsess* is a better word for it."

"Semantics. Anyway, we're always talking about how much they're like you, or like me. How many times have you said that Isaac looks like your dad? Isn't that a big part of why we love them so much?"

I took a sip of wine and considered that. "I don't know. I think it might be part of *how* we love them, but not *why.* With an adopted child, you just have a different *how,* if you see what I mean. You don't love him any less. Just differently, the way we love each of ours differently."

Peter shrugged. "Maybe. I guess we'll probably never know. Anyway, it sounds like you think the adoption might be related to Bobby's suicide."

"If it was a suicide."

"Is there still any doubt? What are the cops saying?"

"I'm not sure, but I think they're still considering it a suspicious death." I told Peter about Bobby's on-line purchases, and he agreed that the behavior didn't sound like that of a man about to kill himself. "Al made another call to one of his friends. I'm hoping he can prod the cops into looking at Bobby's case a little more closely."

"How is Al? How's his new business?"

"Okay, I guess. Oh. Ha. You'll never believe this. It's the most ridiculous thing. He wants me to go into business with him."

Peter looked at me seriously. "Why is that so ridiculous?"

"What? Me, go into business as a private eye? Like Hercule Poirot? Or Cordelia Gray? Or Matlock?"

"I don't think it's such a nutty idea for you to team up with Al to do some investigation. It's clear you have a knack for it, don't you think? Without you, the cops would never have solved Abigail Hathaway's murder or the Fraydle Finkelstein thing. Why *not* turn this skill of yours into a career?"

"Because I *have* a career. Or had one. I don't want another. Anyway, I'm supposed to be home raising the kids, remember?"

He shrugged. "You decided that you couldn't be a half-time public defender. Maybe you could be a half-time investigator."

"It would never work. What would I do? Sit around Al's empty garage helping him polish his gun collection? I have better things to do with my time."

"Like?"

"Like car pool! Like playdates!"

"That reminds me," he said. "Since I'm getting back to work, you get to take Ruby and Isaac to Ari's birthday party tomorrow. I've got a meeting with the studio executive assigned to my project." He reached into his pocket and handed me an invitation printed with a pattern of mottled green, brown, and black.

"Tell me this isn't *camouflage*," I said.

• • •

Is it only in Los Angeles that people would do this? Or is it because Ruby's classmate Ari's parents were from Israel, where they take for granted that the army is a part of life? Whatever the reason, the party was like something out of a movie: *Rambo* or *The Guns of Navarone*. Isaac had never been so happy in his entire life.

The playroom of the birthday boy's house was decorated in brown and green streamers. The party hats perched jauntily on the children's heads were little green berets. G.I. Joe himself was there, though he was actually more of a G.I. Jacob. Ari's uncle, who had recently mustered out of the Israeli army and immediately immigrated to Los Angeles to work in his brother's chain of electronics stores, wore what looked like an Israeli army uniform, complete with sergeant's stripes and a webbed belt cinched tightly at the waist. He had a black plastic toy Uzi submachine gun hanging on his shoulder (at least I hoped it was a toy), and dark red combat boots. His dark, curly hair peeked out from under a burgundy beret that was close in color to his full, pouty lips. He had longer lashes than I did.

The kids marched around the living room in formation for a while, then had a water pistol fight in the backyard. I concentrated my attention on the soldier uncle and did my best to keep from licking my lips. What is it about a man in uniform? No matter how much all of the guns and pageantry of it bothers me, I still find something strangely compelling about a set of cute buns swathed in military green.

At the same time that I was drooling over the soldier, I was feeling pretty damn disgusted about the whole gun thing.

Thank God Stacy was there. Her son Zach was quite a bit older than the birthday boy, but as he went to school with Ari's sister, he'd been invited to join in the festivities. We leaned against the kitchen counter talking softly.

"Can you believe this?" I asked.

She rolled her eyes and flicked back her thick blond hair. Stacy is one of those women who were born to make others feel jealous. She seems beautiful, although she's the first to point out that it's more a result of careful preparation and judicious spending than any natural physical perfection. Her hair is always carefully cut in a classic modification of the style of the moment, and I haven't seen her without makeup since we graduated from college. Her life seems perfect, too. She has a math-whiz son, a handsome husband, and she is one of the rising stars at International Creative Artists, Hollywood's biggest talent agency. Unfortunately, what with her husband Andy's infidelities, sustaining that image of impeccable contentment requires as much work and artifice as does keeping up her physical appearance. She and Andy have been in and out of divorce court and couple's counseling, trying for years to deal with the fact that she earns more money than he does and that, for some reason, that fact instills in him the urge to buy expensive cars and even more expensive women.

"I just don't get it, really I don't. Why are boys so infatuated with guns and soldiers?" I said, keeping my voice low.

"I don't know. Probably because their parents are," Stacy said.

"Are they? Do you really think these people are gun owners?" I waved at the collection of Hollywood and almost-Hollywood parents. The women all looked like they were trying to be Stacy, and the men had that self-satisfied air they tend to acquire when their incomes keep pace with their toy-buying whims.

"You'd be surprised," my friend said.

"Am I going to have to start asking whether there's a gun in the house before I send Ruby and Isaac out on playdates?"

"It's not a bad idea. But, then, Ruby's been over to my house thousands of times. It's never bothered you."

My jaw dropped. "You have a gun?"

She nodded. "Just a little one. I got it last year after Andy moved back home."

"Are you kidding me? Why?"

"Remember last's year's bimbo?"

"Who could possibly keep track?"

Stacy rolled her eyes. "I know, I know. Anyway, she was the craziest of them all. After he broke up with her, she started calling the house at all hours. We changed our phone number, and then she started calling me at work. I kept imagining that scene from *Fatal Attraction*, you know, where Glenn Close puts the bunny in the pot? I wanted to be prepared in case she came after Zach's gerbil."

Was I the only person in the city of Los Angeles who wasn't packing heat?

The pièce de résistance of the party—I swear I'm not making this up—was a piñata shaped like a two-foot-long pistol. The kids thwacked at it happily, while Ari's parents beamed and scrupulously videotaped every minute of the festivities. When the piñata finally burst, after a good half hour of feeble strikes by the children and one good whack with his machine gun by G.I. Jake, a rain of tiny plastic soldiers, water pistols, and foil-wrapped chocolates in the shape of rifle cartridges showered down on the children's heads. God knows where they got the candy bullets.

After cake and ice cream, I gathered my two and put them in the car.

"That was a *gun* party," Isaac announced, beside himself with astonishment and glee.

"Yes, it was. Did you like it?" I asked them.

"I didn't," Ruby said loyally. "We don't like guns, do we Mama?"

"No. No, we don't."

"I do," Isaac said. "I love guns. I *love* them. And I loved that party. That's the kind of party I'm going to have, okay?"

"Over my dead body," I said, thinking of Bobby Katz and what a gun had done to him.

"No!" Isaac wailed.

"What, honey?" I asked, leaning into the car where I'd just buckled him into his car seat.

He wrapped his soft, plump arms around me and kissed me on the cheek, hard. "I don't want you to have a dead body."

I kissed him back. "That's just a saying, honey. My body is fine. It just means I don't want you to have a gun party."

"But why not?" he whined.

"I've told you a million times, baby. Guns are bad; they kill people."

"Real guns are bad. *They* kill people. Play guns are just pretend. They just pretend to kill people."

I looked at him, surprised. Did he, at his age, really understand the difference between real and pretend? "Even pretending to kill people is bad, Isaac."

His lower lip pooched out a bit and his eyes filled with tears. "Am I a bad boy?" he whispered.

"No! No, of course not." I covered him with kisses. "You're a very good boy. You're the best boy."

"Mama?" Ruby interrupted.

"What, sweetie?"

"Well, you always tell Isaac guns are bad. So maybe that's why Isaac thinks *he's* bad. 'Cause he loves something so much, even though it's so bad."

I stared at her. Then I turned to him. "Is that true, Isaac? Do you think you're a bad boy because you love guns and I tell you guns are bad?"

He burst into tears and buried his head in my neck.

Ten

THAT night I finally got around to reading all the E-mail Bobby had received after his death. There were a couple of messages from clients, obviously written before they knew what happened to him. The rest were from Internet contacts who were not aware that he'd died. There were messages from his on-line adoptee support group. There were piles of spam—junk mail from mortgage brokers and pornography web sites and the like. Mostly, however, there were messages from Candace.

The first of Candace's messages began with a plaintive lament about his failure to contact her. Apparently, it had been a long time since she'd received an E-mail from him. She begged him not to cut her out of the "loop of his life." The rest of the message had to do with the letter Bobby had written his birth mother. Candace urged him to ignore the woman's failure to respond and to contact her. Candace's tone was almost nagging. Clearly, she'd been giving him this advice for some time. At one point she even threatened to "drive out there" and talk to the woman herself. I didn't think she was serious, the words were followed by a keyboard ;), but the threat didn't strike me as entirely idle.

In her next message, Candace apologized for "haranguing" Bobby and asked him to call her or come by the café. After that came a string of short messages. A couple begged him to call and apologized again and again for "being so bossy." Finally, she grew angry and called him cruel and selfish for excluding her from "the most important moment of your life—the culmination of your very existence."

There followed twenty or so one-line messages along the lines of "Where are you?" and "Why aren't you answering me?"

The last message began with the words, "You know I love you." It went on from there. She told him that long before they'd met in person she'd realized that she wanted to dedicate herself to him. She insisted that their shared tragedy brought them together. She berated him for his unwillingness to consider a relationship with her, his obvious "soul mate." Finally, she wrote, "I know you say that the reason you don't want to be with me—in every sense of the word— is because you consider me your 'soul sister,' and not your lover. But we both know that's not true. You're allowing your guilt about Betsy to keep you from realizing your true destiny. The Lakota don't believe that you can hide from your destiny. You can't remain shackled to that stoned and destructive soul, not when mine cries out to you."

I leaned back in my chair with a sigh. Poor Candace. Poor Bobby. The truth was, he seemed an unlikely object of such passionate devotion. Bobby had been handsome, sure, but in a kind of bland, blond way. His good looks were strained, blurred, somehow, as a result, I'd always assumed, of his methamphetamine use—speed wreaks havoc on the skin. Bobby was, of course, in good shape. It was his job to be. He wasn't, however, bulky and overly defined. He had a pleasantly strong and firm body, and his stomach was less of a washboard than a solid countertop. But really what made him seem something less than a Lothario was his easygoing, almost innocuous manner. He was pleasant and cheerful. He was ready with an encouraging word or an inspiring quote from one of his AA manuals. But he wasn't passionate. He wasn't ardent or fervent. He was calm and pleasant and de-cidedly un–soul mate–like. But then, who am I to say? My soul mate spends most of his days playing with vintage ac-tion figures and writing about serial murder, cannibalism, and human sacrifice.

THE next morning, Al called me with the news that he had, basically, no news. His sources at the LAPD weren't saying much about Bobby's death.

"Let me put it this way," Al said. "It could be suicide. Or maybe not. I get the feeling they're thinking that if it was a homicide, it was a drug hit—you knew the guy was an addict, right?"

"Recovered."

"Whatever. Once an addict always an addict, that's what I say."

I rolled my eyes at the phone. "How original, Al."

"Anyway, the gun wasn't registered to him or to anyone else, but there's no evidence it was an illegal weapon. It was most likely purchased through a gun show, in which case there would be no records about who bought it."

"Why not? Don't gun sellers have to do background checks?"

"Not at gun shows."

"Why not?"

Al didn't answer for a moment. Then he said, "Honestly, I've never really understood that myself. Anyway, a background check wouldn't do us much good. Those records are destroyed after the person passes the check."

"What?" I was shocked. "Why? Why destroy the record of who bought the gun?"

"Haven't you heard of privacy, girlie? You want the United States government keeping track of its private citizens' every move?"

"I sure as hell want the government keeping track of the gun buyers!" I said.

I could feel Al seething on the other end of the line. Finally, he said, "Listen, you tree-hugging feminist, I'm just *not* going to have this fight with you. And, anyway, maybe you should be *thanking* me instead of *yelling* at me."

I was suitably rebuked and decidedly chastened. "You're right. Thank you so much. Really. Don't be mad, okay?"

He sighed. "No sweat. It's not your fault. You're confused.

Anyway, I got the skip trace results back on the two women
from the hospital. I'li fax them over to you."

"Thanks. Really. I owe you one."

"Don't owe me. Come work with me."

I laughed.

"I'm not kidding," he said.

I'D already figured that the younger woman, Brenda Fessler,
was the mom. I knew that Bobby had been adopted through
Jewish Family Services, and Fessler sounded like a Jewish
name. Moreover, I thought a nineteen-year-old was more
likely to put up a child for adoption than a twenty-six-year-
old. The skip trace had turned her up in Reno, Nevada. I
tried the telephone number but found it disconnected. I
tapped my fingers on the table for a moment, irritated at
the dead end. Then, figuring what the heck, I could afford
the ninety cents, I called information. There was no Brenda
Fessler listed, but there was a Jason Fessler. I decided to give
it a whirl. The phone rang once and was picked up by a
jaunty voice. I wasn't really expecting much, but when I
asked for Brenda the man yelled out, "Hey, Ma! Now you're
getting *phone calls* at my house! Here, give me the baby."

"Hello?" The voice was as bright and cheerful as the
man's, and I hoped that this might be the woman I was
looking for.

"Hi. I hope you can help me. I'm trying to track down
the mother of a baby boy born at Haverford Memorial Hospital on February 15, 1972."

"Again?"

"Excuse me?" I asked.

"A nice young man called me about this very thing a month or so ago. He was born on that date and was trying to find his mother. Are you calling about the same baby?"

"Yes, I am."

"Well, I'll tell you what I told him. Much as I wish I could help him, he's not mine. My Jason was born at Haverford Memorial on February 15, 1972, and he's right here. You called his house, actually. And I'm holding his son, Jason Jr., who's six months old. And a doll. Aren't you? A big precious doll?" I thanked the happy grandmother for her time and hung up.

It had to be Susan Masters. The skip trace had turned up a woman whose maiden name was Susan Masters but whose married name was Sullivan. The fact that confused me was that the date of her name change was 1968, a full four years before Bobby was born. The birth date and the social security number matched, however. For some reason, Susan Sullivan had used her maiden name when she checked into the hospital. Perhaps because she planned to give her baby up for adoption and hoped for some anonymity.

The Sullivans still lived in Los Angeles. Their address was in the Pacific Palisades, a beautiful little community north of Santa Monica. I dialed the number, and a woman's voice answered almost immediately.

"Hello, I'm looking for Susan Sullivan."

"This is she." Did I imagine a whiff of suspicion in her tone?

"Mrs. Sullivan, I'm trying to track down the mother of a baby boy born in Haverford Memorial Hospital on February 15, 1972—"

The phone clicked before I'd even finished my sentence. I was talking to empty air. I tried again, hoping that we'd just been disconnected, but the phone rang and rang. Susan Masters Sullivan did not want to be found. But found she was. I was determined to talk to her and see if she had any information about Bobby's death, whether she wanted to see me or not.

Unfortunately, I also had to go pick Ruby up from preschool. Isaac, who'd been napping while I made my calls, didn't even stir when I hoisted him out of bed, flung him over my shoulder, and hauled him out to the car. The boy had slept about twenty minutes in the entire first four months of his life, turning me into a blithering idiot and putting a strain on my marriage the likes of which we'd never experienced before or since. Now a brass band wouldn't wake him up.

I was only seven minutes late picking up Ruby, a personal record, but nonetheless I found her tapping her foot, arms folded across her narrow little chest. I ignored her irritation and said, "Let's get moving, kid. You and Isaac need to go home and play with Daddy."

"Why? I want to play with *you*."

"Sorry, Ruby. I'm busy this afternoon."

"What are you doing?"

I certainly wasn't going to say, "Investigating a murder." So I settled for, "I've got a playdate."

That seemed to satisfy my daughter.

I don't know why, but I was expecting Susan Sullivan to live in one of the cute little bungalows on the tree-lined streets in Pacific Palisades. I knew once I saw the address that her house was going to be worth something, but even those little cottages sell for a cool million bucks in today's overinflated real estate market. What I didn't expect, however, was a mansion. I didn't expect a house set so far back off the street that its driveway had a Private Road sign. I didn't expect a curving drive of crushed pink gravel, lawns and gardens as far as the eye could see (at least up to the boundary rows of fragrant eucalyptus trees), or the glimpse of a marble-bordered pool peeping out from behind one wing of the salmon-stuccoed villa. I cringed as the wheels of my Volvo station wagon crushed the carefully combed stones and marred the manicured perfection of the circular driveway.

Rich people make me nervous. I rummaged around in my purse for some makeup, found an old lipstick, and carefully applied it. I looked for something to cover the triangle of pimples that had taken up residence on my chin, cursing yet again the acne gods who didn't even allow a single moment of bliss between blemishes and wrinkles. I'd gone from having one to having both with nary a day of smoothness in between.

I fluffed up my cropped curls, relieved that at least I'd remembered to have my roots done, and firmly averted my eyes from the chocolate milk stain down one leg of my khaki capri pants. I was ready to see how the other half lived.

I rang the bell, listening to the chimes echo throughout

the house. The door was answered by an older Mexican woman in a plain gray smock.

"Yes?" she said.

"*Buenos días. Estoy buscando la señora de la casa, Mrs. Sullivan.*"

The woman flashed me a huge smile brightened by at least four silver teeth along the side of her mouth and, with a cascade of Spanish far beyond my limited skills, ushered me through the door and into a round entry hall. The ceiling was easily twenty or thirty feet tall and opened into a massive, round skylight of leaded stained glass. Little oblongs of brightly colored light glowed on the polished marble floor and up the circular staircase along the back wall.

Within a few moments, the maid returned, following behind a tall blond woman wearing a white tennis dress with mint-green piping. Her bobbed hair was colored strawberry blond, as if she were matching the hair color she'd had as a girl. She looked like a blonde. Not a tanned, California surfer-girl kind of blonde but a pallid, English-lass kind of blonde. She had the faded prettiness so common in women of that coloring. She might have once been beautiful, but her skin had crumpled, and her chin seemed to have slipped back into her neck. Her nose, though, was sharp and defined. Her close-set, pale blue eyes glanced at me nervously, as if she knew me and had anticipated my arrival with trepidation.

"Can I help you?" she said. She sounded as though what she really wanted to do was throw me out of her house.

"Mrs. Sullivan, I don't mean to cause you any trouble, and

I'm terribly sorry for bothering you. But my friend Bobby Katz is dead, and I think you can help me."

Susan looked quickly at the maid, who kept her eyes firmly affixed to the floor.

"That will be all, Salud," Bobby's birth mother dismissed her maid, her voice just the tiniest bit hesitant, as if asking the older woman's permission to assert the authority her status ought to have made natural to her.

"I bring you some *limonada,* Mrs. Susan? Some ice tea?" Salud asked.

"No. No, thank you," Susan said. Salud left, and Susan finally met my eye.

"We can't talk out here. Come into the living room," she murmured.

The living room was a vast open space reached through two oversized doors of heavy carved wood. The long gallery opened along one side to a flagstone patio that ran the length of the house. The many sets of French doors were closed against the late-afternoon chill.

She sat down on a button-back armchair and motioned me toward the matching leather sofa. The buttery soft skin felt delicious against the backs of my legs. I introduced myself and told her how I knew Bobby.

"You said he's dead?" she asked in a soft voice.

"Yes. I'm sorry. He died a couple of weeks ago."

"How?"

"It's not clear at this point. He was shot, but the police have not determined yet whether it was suicide or . . . or murder."

She nodded and then began fiddling with the diamond and gold tennis bracelet on her wrist.

"Mrs. Sullivan, I believe you met Bobby," I said.

"He contacted me. As you did. It was you who called, wasn't it?"

I nodded.

"He contacted me. But I told him what I'll tell you. I didn't give birth to a baby in 1972. I'm not his mother. He made a mistake."

I considered that possibility. Could the skip trace have led to the wrong person? It had been known to happen. But if that were the case, why was she so very nervous?

"There doesn't seem to be any doubt, Mrs. Sullivan. The woman who gave birth to Bobby had your name and used your social security number and birth date."

She kept her eyes on her bracelet, catching bits of light with the diamonds and sending them skittering across the walls.

"There's been a mistake. I'm sorry," she insisted.

I didn't say anything.

Suddenly she stood up and crossed the room. "See," she said, grabbing a double frame with pictures of two young blond men. "These are my boys. P. J. was born in 1969, and Matthew in 1974. I was married in 1968. Why ever would I have given my baby up for adoption?"

I looked at the pictures of the young men. They were both blond and blue-eyed. And they looked quite a bit like Bobby.

I raised my eyebrows at Susan. We both jumped when a

shrill ring pierced the silence like a siren. Moments later, Salud came into the living room, holding a cordless phone.

"It's Mr. Patrick, Mrs. Susan," she said.

"Excuse me," Susan took the phone from her and walked quickly out of the room.

"Can I get you a *limonada*, miss?" Salud asked.

"That would be lovely," I said, and she followed Susan out the door.

I got up and started looking over the photographs perched on the grand piano and on the many bookcases and end tables. I crossed the room to get a better look at a large, glass-enclosed cabinet. In it, I found photographs of men in uniform, fatigues, and camouflage hats. A few of the photos showed soldiers holding large machine guns, the sun beating down on their shirtless backs. Vietnam.

A small glass case resting inside the cabinet held a medal. I looked closer. A Purple Heart. I wondered exactly when it was that Patrick Sullivan had served in Southeast Asia. Had he been over there in, say, June of 1971, nine months before Bobby was born?

I heard Susan's voice in the hall. "Take the phone, Matthew."

A petulant male voice said, "No. I don't want to talk about it."

"Matthew. Your father wants to talk to you. Take the phone."

"I said no. I don't need to hear what he has to say. He's been yelling at me for, like, two days. Anyway, I have to get to work."

"Matthew, honey. Please," she said, plaintively.

"Screw him. And screw you, too."

The front door slammed, and Susan walked slowly back into the room.

She immediately realized that I couldn't have helped but overhear what she'd said. "My son Matthew," she explained. "He and his father are having a disagreement."

I did my best to smile sympathetically. "So, Mrs. Sullivan, was your husband in the military?"

"Yes. He was an Air Force pilot. An Academy graduate," she said, as though by rote.

"He served in Vietnam?"

"Yes. I'm sorry about your friend. Really. But I can't help you. I'm afraid I have to go now. I'm late for my match." She walked quickly out the door and across the hallway. She opened the door and stood, waiting. Unable to think of a way to make her talk to me, I gathered my bag and left. As I walked out, I saw Salud walk out of a door in the back hall holding a tall tumbler, its sides dewed and a sprig of mint carefully balanced on the top. The maid caught my eye, shrugged, and then took a long sip from the glass.

Eleven

MAJOR Patrick Sullivan had served two tours of duty in Vietnam in the early seventies. In September of 1972, he'd been shot down over North Vietnam but had managed to work his way back to friendly territory, despite suffering two broken shoulders and severe burns on his hands. He was discharged not long after. The archive of the L.A. Times was full of stories describing his triumphant return, including one photograph of a much younger Susan Sullivan, wearing a pink pillbox hat and crouching next to two small boys as Major Sullivan ran across the tarmac toward them.

A little more searching in on-line news files showed stories about the Sullivan family of Los Angeles and Santa Barbara, going back as far as the archives would take me. One piece, an obituary of a Patrick Sullivan who died in 1980 at the age of seventy-three, was most instructive. Patrick Sr., Major

Sullivan's dad, had been, like his son after him, a pilot in the United States Air Force. He himself was described as a scion of an old California family that had earned its money during the gold rush and later on as real estate barons. He was an intimate friend of Archbishop Timothy Manning and an important member of the Catholic community. He was survived by his son Major Sullivan and his two grandsons, Patrick Jr. and Matthew, and by his brother, Father Edward Sullivan, provost of Saint Ignatius University. His will included a bequest described as "generous" to that Jesuit institution. A wing of the physical sciences building had been named in his honor.

With a husband away at war and the reputation of a prominent Catholic family to consider, no wonder Susan Sullivan had, when she found herself pregnant, given birth in secret and given the baby up for adoption. It was curious, however, that she gave the baby up to a *Jewish* adoption service.

The next morning, I stopped by Betsy's house. She was home, and I got the feeling that that's pretty much where she'd been since I'd seen her last. She wasn't high, or at least she didn't seem it. I found her watching television, wearing a pair of sweatpants that were clearly much too big for her and a man's flannel shirt. Her hair stood up in odd clumps on her head. She had a huge mug of something steaming in her hand.

"Want a mocha?"

"Sure," I said. I wheeled a snoozing Isaac into the living room and put him in a corner, far away from the blaring television. I'd schlepped him, strapped into his stroller, up the stairs to the apartment. Despite the few times I'd clunked him against the banister, and despite Jerry Springer's theme music, he slept on, blessedly still wedded to his morning nap.

I watched as Betsy puttered around the galley kitchen. She poured a packet of hot cocoa mix and a heaping teaspoonful of instant coffee into a mug, drowned the mess in milk, and microwaved it. She garnished it with a dollop of Cool Whip. I gagged as I took my first sip. I didn't see Betsy having a career at Starbucks in her future.

"Mm. Delicious," I said.

"It's my idea of comfort food. I've been pretty much living on these for the last couple of days. Ever since I took those . . . those . . . you know. That day you saw me. Eating kind of makes me sick, but I'm desperate for sugar. And I need the caffeine. I already sleep like twelve hours a night, even with, like, eight of these a day." Betsy spoke in a listless monotone. She looked and sounded like the before character in a TV commercial for Prozac.

"Honey," I said. "I don't mean to pry, but have you considered seeing someone? Maybe a grief counselor? It sounds to me like you're pretty seriously depressed."

She shook her head. "The last thing I need is some shrink raking through my private business."

Now why would that be? "Well, have you been to a meeting since you took the pills?" She might not be able to say the words, but I sure could.

She shrugged, slurping loudly from her cup. "Not really,

but they're kind of coming to me. Every reformed drunk and stoner I know keeps dropping by to tell me to 'hang tough.' Like they have a clue. Losers."

I set my mug down on the coffee table where it joined four or five other encrusted cups. "Betsy, don't you think that those people might be just the ones who *do* have a clue? Some of them must have experienced the challenge of staying sober in the face of tragedy."

She rolled her eyes.

"What about work? When do you have to go back?" I asked.

"I'm not going back."

"What?"

"I quit my job. I've always hated it, and I don't see why I should bother now. Even though Bobby's family stole all my stuff and is tossing me out of my home, I was smarter than they were about at least some things."

This kind of belligerence was a side of Betsy I hadn't seen before. I tried not to be judgmental. I tried to remember my Kübler-Ross. Wasn't anger a stage of grief through which everyone passed?

"Really?" I said, in a neutral tone.

"Yup. Like our wedding account. Even though we always kept our money separate, we had a joint account set up for wedding expenses. Bobby's parents didn't know about it, because I guess they thought my parents were going to foot the bill for the wedding—like that would ever happen. As soon as I realized those cheapskates were going to Je—bleed me dry, I emptied the money out of that account."

Had she really been about to say "Jew me?"

"How much was in it?" I asked. The question was clearly none of my business, but that didn't seem to bother Betsy.

"Almost fifteen grand. And the best part is that most of it wasn't even mine. I mean, when we first set up the account, I put in about five thousand, but then I had to use that to pay for that fancy lawyer you sent us to. So that whole fifteen thousand came from Bobby's savings, and I got every dime of it. Which is exactly what he would have wanted. I know it." She took another slurp of her concoction, looking very satisfied with herself.

To people like Bobby's parents, fifteen thousand dollars was a fairly meaningless amount of money. But it was enough cash to convince Betsy that she could take some time off work.

Betsy drained her cup and looked over at me. There was a smear of chocolate on her upper lip, and I could barely resist the urge to reach into my purse for a baby wipe and clean it off.

"What have you found out? Did you get any dirt on the creepy Katzes?"

I was getting more and more uncomfortable with the vitriol Betsy was spewing in the direction of her would-have-been in-laws. Granted, they hadn't behaved very well toward her. But, at the same time, she seemed to be almost enjoying her anger at them. "No," I said. "But that really wasn't the kind of thing we were looking into, was it?"

She shrugged again.

"I think I found Bobby's birth mother, though."

That perked her up. "Really? Who is she? Did he meet her? What's she like? Is she married? What does her husband do? Do they seem like they've got money?"

Now Betsy was really making me uneasy. Why was she interested in Bobby's mother's financial situation? I was loath to tell her more than I absolutely had to. I told myself that she wasn't technically a client of mine; I didn't owe her any kind of duty, fiduciary or otherwise. I was just a friend of Bobby's looking into his life to see if I could shed some light on his death.

"Why don't I check things out a little more, and when I'm sure it's really her, I'll let you know, okay?" I said.

"Whatever," Betsy said, seeming to lose interest.

ISAAC woke up as I bumped him down the steps to the curb, and he started whining as soon as I loaded him into his car seat. Not even his favorite tape, *The Coasters' Greatest Hits*, calmed him down. I decided to strike a bargain. I promised him half an hour at the playground if he promised to behave afterward and let me take him with me on a grown-up playdate.

As soon as we crossed from sidewalk to sand, Isaac made a beeline for the tire swing. Since the little girl who was sitting in it didn't want to give up her perch, he shoved her off. I ran over, scooped her up, and handed her to her mother, who snatched her out of my arms. I put Isaac in a time-out, which he didn't seem to mind particularly. I released him on condition that he figure out a way to "share." He did.

He "shared" another child's shovel by wrenching it out of the little boy's hands, aiming it at his head, and shouting, "Bang, bang, you're a dead man!" Then he poked the kid with the shovel. Hard.

Within two minutes, my precious boy and I were relegated to a sandy patch of unpopulated lawn on the far corner of the playground. I smiled pathetically at the mothers whose scowls had precipitated our segregation and called, "I have a really well-behaved daughter." I swear it wasn't my fault my son was behaving like a testosterone-poisoned member of the World Wrestling Federation. The mothers shot me final, disgusted looks and formed themselves into a protective circle around their perfectly behaved children, many of whom were boys, no doubt raised by more competent mothers who could effectively resist gender stereotypes.

Meanwhile, my monstrous son had crawled into my lap and was placing firm but gentle kisses all over my face.

"You are my darling," he said to me.

"You're my darling, too, but I wish you wouldn't attack the other kids." I sighed, kissing him back. His cheeks and neck still had the doughy softness of infancy, and I buried my nose in them. He giggled while I made snuffling noises and buzzed at his soft skin with my lips. How could something so delicious be so wretchedly behaved?

We played in our corner for a while and then made our way over to the slide. Two mothers promptly grabbed their little girls and carried them to the other side of the park. Isaac, blissfully unaware of his pariah status, clambered up the ladder and whizzed down the slide with a bellow of joy.

Was it really just a matter of gender? For all her stub-
borness, for all her temper and propensity to willful behavior, Ruby was, by and large, an obedient child. Sure she had
her moments, but they'd never included socking a kid on
the head with a piece of playground equipment. Isaac, who
had once seemed so tractable and still amazed me with his
loving sweetness, had an exuberant, aggressive streak about
the length and breadth of the Mississippi River—with the
same tendency to overflow. I'm convinced that neither Peter
nor I treated them any differently from one another. So what
was it? The mysterious Y chromosome? Or maybe it was
just Isaac. Maybe that's the way the kid was, and all my
efforts at forcing him to be something else, forcing him to
be more like his sister, were not only hopeless but ultimately
destructive. Maybe instead of trying to beat and berate out
of him that wonderful sparky personality that gave me such
joy when it wasn't being unleashed on unsuspecting children, I should have been helping him figure out how to
direct it more appropriately. Like at inanimate objects.

At the end of our agreed-upon half-hour, Isaac was happy to
leave, the attractions of solitary play having worn thin. I
strapped him back in the car seat, popped the ubiquitous
Coasters into the cassette deck, and set off for the Palisades. It
never occurred to me not to bring Isaac on this errand. First of
all, I had nowhere else to put him. Peter had spent the entire
night working on *The Impaler* and probably wouldn't wake up
until the sun was dipping back down in the horizon. Equally
important to me, however, was a somewhat less innocent motive. There is something about a mother and toddler that in-

spires the sharing of confidences. Any woman who's ever taken a baby to the playground can attest to that. Mothers tell things to one another even when they've never met before. I can't count the number of times I've been made privy to a virtual stranger's innermost secrets while our children cavorted on the swing set. I'll admit that with the Ninja Toddler around, I'd been less often the sounding board for other women's intimacies than I had been with a sweet-faced Ruby on my lap, but since Susan Sullivan didn't have a little boy for Isaac to torment, I figured I was safe.

Either Bobby's birth mother lived in tennis whites, or it was just a coincidence that I'd caught her on her way to the courts once again. This time Salud didn't ask me in but made Isaac and me wait on the doorstep. Susan herself looked as though she were about to send me packing, but her face softened when she saw Isaac's tousled head. He didn't have his sister's dramatic red ringlets, but his sandy blond hair still highlighted his deceptively cherubic face.

"Why don't you come round to the back?" she said. "There's a swing set out there. It belonged to my boys when they were young, and I've never had the heart to take it down. I guess I'm saving it for grandchildren."

She led us around the side of the house. As we walked across the lawns, I was conscious of my clogs sinking deep in the lush, damp grass. The back yard was expansive and as perfectly groomed as the front. Flower beds flanked a large grassy area edged with blue and gray stones. A green climbing structure, complete with swings, tree house, and sandbox, stood in a generous patch of playground bark. As soon as he saw it, Isaac took off for it at a run.

"He won't hurt himself," Susan said. "The bark is about a foot deep. I still replace it every spring."

She led me to two Adirondack chairs set at the edge of the huge flagstone patio, and we watched Isaac in silence for a moment or two. He was in heaven, climbing up the rope ladder, sliding down the firefighter's pole.

"You came back," Susan said finally.

"Yes," I replied.

"Why?"

"Your husband was stationed overseas, in Vietnam, when Bobby was born."

She didn't answer, simply rolled her diamond tennis bracelet around and around her wrist.

"I imagine it must have been very difficult, finding yourself pregnant under those circumstances, especially considering who his family was." I kept my voice gentle, but I don't believe it was my tone, or anything I said or did, that made Susan Masters Sullivan finally speak. She told me her story because she desperately wanted to talk to someone. Her son was dead, and whether or not she'd ever known him, she felt some kind of grief, and she needed someone to share it with.

"I'm sorry he's dead. I really am," Susan said, without looking at me. Her voice had a huskiness to it, and I wondered if she was suppressing tears.

"Yes," I said. "We all are. He was a lovely man."

"I didn't know him well enough to tell. You see, we met just the once."

I didn't speak. I was afraid that if I did, she would stop talking. I realized that I was holding my breath, and I let it out as quietly as I could.

"I was twenty-six years old when I had him. I had been married for almost three years. My family . . . well, they weren't much. My dad moved us out here from Chicago because of Santa Anita. You know, the racetrack? He'd been a groom at a racing stable in Saratoga, New York, and he thought he'd make a career out of horse training. But anything he earned at the stables, he'd lose at the betting window or drink up on his way home at night. My mother supported us. She was a dispatcher for a taxicab company."

Susan glanced at my face and looked away almost immediately.

"I'm not telling you my hard luck story because I want you to feel sorry for me. It's just that all this had a lot to do with what happened. You see, when I met my husband, it was like meeting a prince from a completely different world. And I was Cinderella. He was home from the Air Force Academy for Christmas. We met at a fraternity party at USC, and for the longest time he thought I was a student there. I didn't ever really lie, I just didn't correct his misunderstanding. When he graduated and began his service, he came home so rarely . . . I guess I sort of stopped thinking about what he knew or didn't know. We got married, in kind of a hurry. For the usual reason. It was only then that he found out that I wasn't a college girl but . . . some other kind of girl. But it was too late.

"I think his parents always knew that I wasn't what I

seemed to be. They never liked me. Not back then, and not after the kids were born. They set me up in a little house in Beverly Hills while Patrick was overseas. They paid all my bills. Mary-Margaret even took me to her very own obstetrician. They hired a baby nurse for P. J. I almost felt like Mary-Margaret was teaching me how to be a Sullivan—like she was training me to be the kind of wife she wished Patrick had married.

"I suppose I felt smothered. Or else I was lonely. It's funny, that you can feel so oppressed by people's expectations and demands, but still so desperately alone."

I nodded in sympathy. I'd felt something similar when I'd first had Ruby. Sometimes I thought that having a baby was the most lonely thing in the world. There you are, constantly at another person's beck and call, never by yourself for even a minute, but utterly isolated and alone.

"I met Bobby's father at Papa Bach's Bookstore. I used to hide out there, sometimes, when the nanny came. I was terribly intimidated by her. She so clearly disapproved of how little I knew about being a mother. I just know she was telling Mary-Margaret everything I did wrong. Anyway, I was there one morning, and this nice young man kept watching me. After a while he asked me out for a cup of coffee. I don't know why I went. Like I said, I guess I was lonely. Anyway, we had coffee and talked. He was a doctor. A pediatrician. He was handsome—I mean, not like Patrick, not blond and gorgeous—but kind of dark and moody looking. He was a Jew, and I hadn't really known many Jews. I went to Catholic schools through high school, and I never really did go to college.

"Anyway, we met at Papa Bach's a few times, and then, one afternoon, I went home with him. I don't know why. I never could figure out why. I just did. It was stupid. But it was 1971. People did things like that. Or at least, I thought they did. It would have been nothing, I would have forgotten all about it." A deep red flush crept up her neck and into her cheeks. "The . . . the rubber broke," she whispered.

I nodded again.

She paused for a moment, cleared her throat, and continued in a stronger voice. "And there I was. Pregnant. I really didn't know what to do. I thought for a while about trying to lie to Patrick and his family. Mary-Margaret and Pat Sr. had flown me out to Japan for a week a month or so before all this happened so that I could meet Patrick for his leave. I suppose I could have pretended I'd gotten pregnant then. But, you see, I knew that chances were I'd be found out. I just knew it."

"Why?" I asked. "Why were you so sure?"

She flushed again and looked out across the yard to where Isaac was lying on his stomach on the bark, digging a pit with his toes. "Well, for one thing, the dates would have been all wrong; the baby would have ended up coming a whole month late. Although he ended up coming a week or so early, so I guess I could have worked it out somehow. Maybe I could have gone away to have him and just lied about his age by a couple of weeks. But there was something else."

"What?"

"Well, like I said, the man was . . . Jewish. And he looked Jewish. You know. Dark."

I was waiting for her to remark on the size of her lover's nose, but she refrained. I suppose it had occurred to her at some point that Applebaum wasn't exactly a WASPy name.

"You didn't think you'd be able to get away with it?"

"No. I thought for sure Patrick would be able to tell."

"It's ironic," I said.

"What is?"

"Well, that Bobby was so blond. He looks just like his half brothers."

She nodded. "He did, didn't he? They all three favor me. But, then, I couldn't be sure that he would. Favor me, that is. What if he'd looked like his father?"

I nodded.

"And thank God I did it, given what happened," she said.

"Excuse me?"

"You know, that Tay-Sachs. The Jewish disease. Even if I'd been able to keep it a secret from Patrick, he would have found out, because Bobby had that Jewish genetic disease."

"Well, chances are that you wouldn't have found out about the Tay-Sachs," I said.

"Why not?"

"Bobby only got tested because he was Jewish. If he'd been brought up as your child, there never would have been a reason for him to be tested. Unless he married a Jewish girl."

"I doubt a son of mine would do that," she said and then stiffened as if suddenly remembering who or what I was. "I mean, they don't meet many Jewish people. They went to Catholic schools. Like my husband and I did. But even so, we would have found out."

"How?"

"Because we were all tested for it a few years ago."

"Excuse me?" I was flabbergasted. She'd have had no reason in the world to be tested for Tay-Sachs.

"My sister's granddaughter has cystic fibrosis. Her doctors at UCLA asked the entire family to participate in a genetic study. We were all tested."

"What do you mean? What does being tested for cystic fibrosis have to do with Tay-Sachs?"

"Because the test they gave us was what they call a panel. It looked for three diseases at once, cystic fibrosis, Tay-Sachs, and something else, caravan? Canavan? I can't remember the name. Anyway, they used that panel for the entire study, and even though we weren't in a risk group, we had to be tested like everyone else. My test came back positive for cystic fibrosis, P. J.'s and Matthew's tests were negative. Of course none of us had the Tay-Sachs gene or the one for that other Jewish disease. If Bobby's had come back positive for Tay-Sachs, then Patrick would have found out he wasn't his child, that his father was someone else, someone Jewish."

"I guess you're right, then. You were lucky." I glanced over at Isaac, who was digging a hole in the wood chips. He looked happy, so I turned back to Bobby's mother. "How did you keep your pregnancy a secret?"

"It was surprisingly easy. Even though P. J. was already a year and a half old, I was still carrying quite a bit of my pregnancy weight. I just kept wearing the same clothes and tried not to eat too much. I didn't end up gaining more than twenty pounds or so."

I stared at her jealously. *Twenty pounds? I gained that much in the first trimester!*

"No one really noticed," she continued. "At the end, I stayed in bed a lot. I told the nanny that I was having migraines. Mary-Margaret made me go to her doctor, and I was terrified that the jig would be up, but he didn't look at me past my neck. He just prescribed some sleeping pills and sent me home. It was only in the very last month that it was really obvious that I was pregnant. I sent P. J. off to Mary-Margaret and Pat Sr. I told them I was going to Arizona to a spa to try to lose weight once and for all before Patrick came home on leave again. They bought it. I think they were glad to have me gone for a little while.

"Instead, I went home to my mother in Pasadena and had the baby at Haverford Memorial Hospital. I registered as Susan Masters, and that was that. I gave the baby to Jewish Family Services and went home."

"Why did you go through Jewish Family Services and not through one of the Catholic agencies?"

"My mother wanted me to go through a Catholic charity. In fact, she tried to convince me to go to Saint Anne's Maternity Home, this home for unwed mothers in Los Angeles. But I wasn't unwed. I didn't belong there. And I had to give the baby to the Jews."

"Why?" I asked again.

"The baby was half-Jewish, wasn't he? It didn't seem fair to try to give a half-Jewish baby to Catholic family."

"Fair?"

"Well, because they were sure to assume he was from a

Catholic family, because of me, because of my name. But he'd be part Jewish."

I didn't get it. "So what?"

"Well, they'd end up with a Jewish baby. That wouldn't be right."

I stared at her for a moment, not sure what to say. Was she really saying that she couldn't stomach the idea of foisting off a Jewish baby on an unsuspecting Catholic family? As if they'd be getting inferior goods?

My discomfort didn't seem to register on Susan in the slightest. She gave me the name of Bobby's birth father, Dr. Reuben Nadelman, and told me that she'd given it to Bobby, too, but had never found out whether Bobby had contacted him.

While I was writing Bobby's birth father's name on a scrap of paper, I heard Isaac squeal. I looked up, and my heart caught in my throat. For a moment, I thought that the handsome blond young man pushing my son on the swing was Bobby. Susan Sullivan followed my gaze.

"My son, Matthew," she said fondly. "I remember when he was small, like your boy. I used to push him on that very swing."

"He and Bobby look so much alike," I said.

She smiled faintly, and her lip trembled. "Like brothers," she murmured.

"Well, I guess that only makes sense," I said. I felt bad as soon as the words escaped my lips. It seemed cruel to remind her that Bobby had been hers, her son just like this man was. Something about Susan Sullivan inspired me to want to protect her, she seemed so delicate, so fragile. And yet, this was a woman who felt such clear distaste for who I was.

As Isaac and I drove away from the Pacific Palisades, I felt a kind of listless disgust. As the most assimilated of Jews, married to an indeterminate Protestant of vaguely Anglo-Saxon heritage, I gave little thought in my life to anti-Semitism. I'd never been called a kike or a hebe. As far as I knew, I'd never failed to get a job or make a friend because I was a Jew. My life had been blessedly devoid of prejudice. So much so, in fact, that I'd sort of forgotten that there were people in my own country, my own city, for whom my status as a Jew meant something more than that I hung a few Stars of David on our Christmas tree. Susan Sullivan had given away her baby because his father was a Jew. Despite the fact that a conveniently scheduled leave in Japan meant that she might have been able to convince her husband and his family that he had impregnated her, she gave her baby up for adoption. She was *that* sure that his Jewish blood would give him away, that it would mark him, as surely as a pair of horns on the top of his head. I angled the rearview mirror so that Isaac's sleeping face was reflected back at me. Did he look Jewish? Half the blood that flowed through his veins could be traced back to the Jewish Pale in Poland, and farther, if the biblical stories are true, to the rocky, desert sands of Israel. Did his face bear indelible traces of generations of hook-nosed moneylenders?

My son's sand-colored hair stuck to his damp, sweaty fore-head. His blue eyes were closed, and his thick lashes rested

on round, pink cheeks. His soft lips formed the shape of the
nipple he was probably dreaming of. If I were totally honest,
I would allow that his nose was perhaps a little large for his
tiny face. But the fact was, he had inherited that from his
father, whose own visage bore the craggy sail of an oversized
schnoz that could easily have graced the pages of a Nazi
caricature. And there wasn't a Jewish bone in Peter's body.

My grandmother, who'd lived long enough to see us married, had wept at our wedding. I'd assumed it was because
Peter wasn't Jewish, and I'd gone up to her after the ceremony at my mother's urging, prepared to promise to raise
our children Jewish.

"What a waste!" she'd cried, hugging me to her breast.
"Your tiny *piskela* of a shiksa nose, all for nothing."

ISAAC and I left the Palisades and drove crosstown to Ruby's
Jewish preschool. It was something of a relief to be back in
the world I understood, where even the goyim knew when
to call someone a schmuck and how to eat a pastrami sand-
wich.

On the way home, my cell phone rang. I fumbled for it,
coming dangerously close to swerving into the next lane.

"Hello?" I shouted, over the freeway noise and the crackle
of static.

"Hey! Mama! It's dangerous to talk on the phone and
drive. Daddy says so," Ruby bellowed from the backseat.

I ignored both her voice and that of my conscience and
continued my conversation.

"Hello?" I said again.

"Hi. This is Candace. You know, Bobby's friend."

That was something of a surprise. I hadn't expected to hear from her again.

"How did you get this number?" I asked, sounding ruder than I'd intended.

"Your husband gave it to me. I called the number on your business card, and he told me you'd have your cell phone. I hope it's all right. I can call back if it's not a good time."

"No. No. Now's fine," I said, quickly.

"I was just calling to see how you're doing. I mean, with Bobby's case and all."

I flinched. I didn't have a "case" or a client. All I had was a rather unhealthy curiosity.

"Okay. Fine. Is there anything *you* can tell me, Candace?"

"Me? No. I mean, I don't really know anything. I was just wondering if you'd found out more about Bobby's family. His mother. That kind of thing."

I paused for a moment, trying to figure out exactly what the woman was getting at. The last time we'd spoken, she'd been unwilling to tell me anything other than the name of the hospital where Bobby was born, and that was only to keep me from mentioning her involvement to the police. What was she after now?

"I spoke to Bobby's birth mother," I said.

"Really? What's she like? Did he talk to her before he died? Did she know anything about his death?" The questions poured out of her mouth in a frantic tumble.

I didn't answer any of them.

"Candace, did Bobby mention anything to you about his birth father?" I asked.

"His father? No. Why? Did he find him, too? What is his name? Did Bobby contact him?"

I decided not to be forthcoming with her. "I'm not sure. Was there any other reason you called?"

"Actually, there was," she said. The tone of her voice changed—it became conspiratorial. "I've been thinking a lot about Bobby and his suicide. At first I didn't think it was possible that he'd killed himself, but the more I think about it, the more sense it makes to me."

This caught my attention. This was the first time anyone who knew Bobby had said that it was possible that he'd want to kill himself.

"Really?" I asked. "What makes you say that?"

"Well, you know, Bobby and I were very close. Intimate really." She giggled. It was an unpleasant sound. "He confided in me things that he'd never tell to anyone else."

"Like what?" I asked.

"Like how unhappy he was in his relationship. Like how he wanted to leave Betsy but felt like he couldn't."

I slowed down, not wanting my piqued interest to cause me to get into an accident.

"Why couldn't he leave her?"

"Because she was a junky. He felt like if he left her, she might start using again, or worse."

"Worse?"

"You know, like kill herself or something."

"But why would that make *Bobby* kill *himself*?"

"I don't think you really knew Bobby. Not like I did," she said, her voice oily.

"That's probably true. So maybe you can explain to me why Bobby and Besty's problems, if they were having any, would cause him to kill himself."

"Bobby was a special soul. A sensitive soul. We were very alike in that way. That kind of emotional blackmail makes someone like us feel very . . . very trapped. And anxious. I'm sure that is what Bobby was seeing. He lost sight of himself. He lost sight of the others in his life who could give him peace and joy. So he killed himself."

Everything about what Candace was saying rubbed me the wrong way. She and Bobby didn't seem at all alike, and I doubted that their "special souls" had much in common. Furthermore, the woman was clearly in love with Bobby. Of course she would blame Bobby's lover and fiancée for what had happened to him. But did she have a more nefarious motive for her phone call? Was she trying to steer me in the wrong direction? The E-mails she had sent to Bobby after his body was discovered seemed to absolve her from any knowledge of, or involvement in, his death. On the other hand, even though they'd had the ring of honesty to them, it wasn't impossible that they were part of a ruse to establish her ignorance and innocence.

"So you think Bobby killed himself," I said.

"I think it's possible. Although, of course, there's another possibility, too."

"What's that?"

"That Bobby finally decided to leave Betsy once and for all. And that she killed him rather than let him have his freedom."

Twelve

"Do you think cannibals would ever eat their own young, and if so, how would they reproduce?"

It's a mark of the state of both my marriage and my husband's career that Peter's question didn't faze me in the slightest. "I suppose the mama cannibal would only nosh on her own offspring if no other food sources were available," I said after some thought.

"Hmm. Interesting idea. The possibility of a famine-inspired infanticide could lend the second act just that added level of tension that I've been looking for."

We were lying with our legs tangled together on the couch, recuperating from the effort of putting our children to bed. I'd come close to strapping Ruby in with her jump rope or the utility belt from Isaac's Batman costume, but she'd finally consented to lie still and listen to a tape. The strains of "There's No Business Like Show Business" from *Annie Get Your Gun* were just barely audible. She had a big thing for show tunes; her Ethel Merman imitation was almost as good as her dad's.

"I could spend my entire career writing nothing but cannibal movies." Peter sounded absolutely thrilled at the idea.

"Career. What's that?" I said. He poked me in the side with his toe. I noticed that it was sticking out of his sock. "You need new socks."

"I always need new socks. Are we going to have one of our biweekly, 'I need to figure out what I'm doing with my life' discussions? Because if we are, I'm going to need another cup of coffee."

I kicked him back, making sure to dig a little into his side where I knew he was ticklish.

"No. We're not going to have any kind of discussion at all. No talking allowed," I said.

We amused ourselves for twenty minutes with an activity that had gotten entirely too rare once we'd had kids, then clicked on the television. We spent a vacant hour watching the end of a spy thriller we could just vaguely remember having seen not long before. One of the benefits of the exhaustion that accompanies parenting is the ability to watch a movie or read a book again and again without remembering a single important feature of the plot.

The next morning, was Saturday, the one day of the week when Peter wakes up with the kids and I get the morning off. I briefly considered heading back to the gym—I hadn't been there since the morning Bobby's body had been discovered—but I couldn't bring myself to go. It was just too strange and sad to imagine working out there without Bobby. And I was too lazy to work out anywhere else.

I left my family involved in an elaborate game of hide and go seek, which consisted of the kids hiding and then shrieking out their locations while Peter looked for them. "We're in the closet, Daddy! No, the *hall* closet!"

I'd found Dr. Reuben Nadelman in about four minutes on the web. He was an attending physician at Cedars Sinai Medical Center's pediatric oncology unit, and he was in their staff directory. I also found a number of references to him in the L.A. Times, including an announcement of his marriage to a Dr. Larissa Greenbaum, a dermatologist. I couldn't find a residential listing for the Nadelmans or for the Greenbaum-Nadelmans (and people wonder why I don't bother to hyphenate) in the phone book. I launched Lexis, a legal search engine, and input the doctors' names in the real estate database. They had purchased a home on Hollyhock Way in Brentwood four years before, the assessed value of which was $1.2 million dollars. I might not have had his phone number, but I'd easily found his address. The World Wide Web—a nosey Parker's best friend.

As I drove through the stone gateway that marked the beginning of the tony Los Angeles neighborhood made infamous by O. J. Simpson's murderous and ultimately unpunished rage, I mused on the coincidence of Bobby being born to one doctor and then adopted by another. Sometimes it seemed like every Jewish mother but my own had gotten her wish.

I wound my way through tree-lined streets past faux French, faux Spanish, and faux English Tudor palaces. Dr. Nadelman lived in a Cape Cod that looked like it had been swallowing the steroid prescription of an East German swimmer. Bobby had been blessed with a seemingly endless supply of wealthy parents.

I was hoping that on a Saturday morning, at 10:30, the doctors would still be home. They didn't disappoint me.

Bobby's birth stepmother (is there such a term?) led me through the house to a large kitchen papered in yellow roses. Bobby's father was seated at one end of a long Country-French table reading the paper.

"Reuben, this is a friend of Bobby Katz's," Larissa Greenbaum-Nadelman said, steering me toward a chair and putting a cup of unasked-for coffee in front of me. She pushed a sugar bowl and a coffee creamer in the shape of a cow with an open mouth across the table to me and sat down next to her husband.

Dr. Nadelman nodded his head, folded up his newspaper, and extended his hand. "I wondered if someone would come by. I read about Bobby's death in the *Times*. I was so very sorry to hear about it. He seemed like a nice man."

"He was," I said. "I take it that Bobby came to see you."

"No, but he wrote to me, and we spoke on the telephone." Dr. Nadelman took a sip of his coffee. He was a small man with nothing of Bobby's carefully tended musculature. His dark hair was salted white above the ears. It crossed my mind that he looked Jewish, with his dark eyes and heavy eyebrows, but he could as easily have been Italian or Greek.

Then I realized that that kind of thinking was just what I'd found so repellent in Bobby's birth mother.

"Bobby contacted me not long ago. He'd received my name from his birth mother, a woman I knew for a short while many years ago. Both Bobby and his mother were under the impression that I was his genetic father."

"Aren't you?" I asked.

"No, I'm not. When Bobby first wrote to me, I thought that it was possible that I was. After all, I had had a sexual relationship with his birth mother, and we had experienced a failure of birth control. Even then, though, it seemed very unlikely that he was my son."

"Why?" I asked. I was absolutely flummoxed by this turn of events. I had been certain, as Bobby most likely had been, that Reuben Nadelman was his biological father.

His wife interrupted. "You see, Ms. Applebaum, Reuben and I tried for many years to have children. While I had a child from a previous marriage, we never conceived one of our own. Reuben's sperm count was just too low."

Dr. Nadelman nodded. "We finally had our son Nate through artificial insemination of donor sperm," he said. "Now, while it's certainly possible for me to have impregnated Susan—after all, all it takes is one sperm—as I said, it's not particularly likely. I told this to Bobby when he called me. I told him about my infertility, and that it was unlikely, though not impossible, that I was his father."

"Do you mind telling me how he reacted?"

Dr. Nadelman shrugged his shoulders. "He was disappointed, I think. Not because he so desperately wanted to be my son, in particular, but because I think he had been so sure he'd found his father."

"Disappointed enough to kill himself?" I asked.

Again the doctor shrugged. "I'm sorry, I really don't know the answer to that. I didn't know him. Certainly not well enough to make a judgment. But he wasn't distraught when we spoke. In fact, he still seemed to hold out a hope that he was my son, despite what I told him about my fertility issues."

"And you don't know for certain that he wasn't your son. As you said, all it takes is one sperm."

"I didn't know for certain, then. I do know now."

"What do you mean?"

"Bobby told me the story of how he came to find out he was adopted in the first place. His diagnosis as a Tay-Sachs carrier led to his determination that he was the biological son of neither of the people whom he had always known to be his parents."

I nodded. I knew that much.

"For that same reason, I could not possibly be his father."

"Excuse me?"

"Tay-Sachs is an inherited condition. It's autosomal recessive. That means that only if both of a child's parents pass on the affected gene will that child have the fatal disease."

I nodded. I knew all this.

"Tay-Sachs *carriers*, on the other hand, receive an affected gene from only one of their parents. That means that either Bobby's birth mother or father was a carrier and passed that gene on to him. Now, as I'm sure you know, Tay-Sachs is a disease found almost exclusively in Jews of Ashkenazic descent. Thus, the gene must have come from his father, because Bobby's birth mother is about as Jewish as the Pope."

I smiled. The doctor had a sense of humor. Not necessarily a good one, but a sense of humor nonetheless.

"Despite the fact that I am Jewish, I am not a carrier of the Tay-Sachs gene," he said. "As you may or may not be aware, Tay-Sachs testing is not a chromosome analysis like, for example, the kind of testing done for Down's syndrome. The Tay-Sachs test involves the detection of an enzyme. Carriers have about half as much of this enzyme called Hex A in their blood as noncarriers. When Bobby told me about his Tay-Sachs, I went and had a blood test to determine my status. It was negative. I'm not a Tay-Sachs carrier and, thus, cannot be Bobby's father."

I felt completely deflated—just as Bobby would have felt.

"Did you tell Bobby that you weren't his father?"

The doctor shook his head. "I would have called him right away, but I didn't have the opportunity. I read about Bobby's death in the papers the same day I received my test results."

I heaved a sigh. "I guess I'm back to the drawing board. I need to find another Jewish man with whom Susan Sullivan had sex at the same time as she had her affair with you."

"Not necessarily," Larissa said.

"What?" the doctor and I spoke in unison.

"French Canadians and certain Louisiana Cajuns also carry the Tay-Sachs gene."

"Really?" I said. "I didn't know that."

"Neither did I," said her husband. "How did you find this out?"

She patted his hand. "After the boy called, I did a little research. I looked at one or two articles on Tay-Sachs."

"Why?" he asked, his brow wrinkled with concern.

She reached up a hand and touched his cheek. "This was before you got the test results back—before we knew you weren't a carrier. I wondered if the Tay-Sachs might have been the cause of your infertility."

"Why didn't you tell me what you'd discovered?"

She smiled gently. "I was afraid it would hurt you. I didn't want you to think that I was still searching for answers. I didn't want you to think I was still tied up in all those horrible knots, that I was still consumed with our fertility issues the way we both were back then, back before Nate was born."

Reuben hugged his wife to him for a moment. In that flash of intimacy, I felt like I could see the relationship these two people shared: the warmth, the love, the respect and caring. I wished so much that Bobby had found out that he was this gentle man's son. The home made by this father would have been the haven the Katzes could never have provided and that Susan Sullivan would not.

"Bobby's father could be either an Ashkenazic Jew or of French-Canadian or Cajun descent," I said, almost to myself.

I sat for a moment, thinking of Susan and her vehemence. And her anti-Semitism. Suddenly, another thought occurred to me. Perhaps Susan Sullivan had protested too much. She had admitted to me that she'd lied to her husband about her education. Maybe she'd lied about much more. Perhaps she'd lied about the results of her genetic testing.

"Is it possible that you *are* Bobby's father, but that his *mother* passed on the Tay-Sachs gene to him? Maybe *she* has Jewish or French-Canadian ancestry."

He looked at me for a moment, surprise in his eyes. "I suppose it's *possible*," he said softly.

Thirteen

"**W**AIT, *you're* asking *me* for help?" I was astonished. I'd spent so much time, over the past couple of years, begging Al for information and assistance. He'd never once asked me for anything in return, other than to lend a sympathetic ear to his Baroque conspiracy theories.

"Don't make so much of it," he growled on the other end of the phone. "I need a little lesson is all. On mitigation and the death penalty."

I'd unwillingly come straight home from my visit to Dr. Nadelman. What I'd really wanted to do was whip over to the Palisades and shake Susan Sullivan until she told me exactly who Bobby's father was and what was going on. Instead, I'd been treated to a hysterical phone call from my husband. It seemed life on the planet could not continue without a certain lavender tutu that had disappeared off the face of the earth. I described various possible tutu hiding places over the phone, to no avail. Finally, and not a little frustrated, I agreed to come home and search for the offending bit of gauze myself. It took me about three minutes to locate it crumpled in a corner of Ruby's dollhouse, where it had been doing service as the carpet in the master bedroom. I was getting ready to throttle both Peter and Ruby when the phone rang.

"And why do you need my help?" I asked Al.

"Because I took a case, and I want to make sure I'm up on exactly what the hell I should be doing here."

"Details?" I leaned back in the kitchen chair, wrapped the phone cord around my finger, and put my feet up on the table. The kids were in Ruby's room playing Barbie. Peter had retired to his office in a huff and was most likely rearranging his first-series Mego *Star Trek* action figures (still in the original packaging). I could be confident of a few moments of tranquillity.

"It's a death penalty case, and the attorney hired me to replace the mitigation investigator, who went out on maternity leave. Might I say, at this point, that you ladies are never going to get anywhere in your careers if you keep dropping the ball to drop a baby?"

"No, you might not. Okay. So you were hired to help the defense attorney flush out information that will convince the jury to give the guy life without parole and not a lethal injection."

"Exactly. Only I've never done a mitigation case before. The lawyer seems like a decent enough guy, for a lawyer, but he dumped the file in my lap without a heck of a lot of explanation or direction. I want to make sure that I'm investigating the right things. You know, finding things that will actually be useful. No point in coming up with a file full of crap."

"True enough. Okay, here's what I'll do. I'm no expert on the death penalty myself. I'll do a little research, find a couple of articles that describe what specific kinds of things can be used in mitigation of a death sentence, and put it all together for you. When do you need this by?"

"Whenever. Yesterday."

"Seriously."

"Well, you got any time today?"

I cocked an ear to the kids. They'd probably let me do a little legal research. I could always toss them in front of the television if I needed to. With Peter working on a mood, I wasn't going to be able to get away to confront Bobby's birth mother anytime soon, at least not without the kids. And I wasn't about to bring them along to what might end up being a confrontation verging on the ugly.

"Sure, I could put in a couple of hours right now," I told Al.

"Let's do this. Do what you can today, and then meet me tomorrow. There's something I want to show you, anyway." He gave me an address in downtown L.A.

"Where am I meeting you?" I asked him.

"It's a surprise."

•   •   •

THE true surprise was how *nice* all the folks were at the indoor firing range. When I'd pulled up in front of the long, low building painted a pale blue, with an oversized mural of cartoon figures pointing weapons, and saw where it was Al had directed me, I'd had to cool off for a few minutes before going inside. Al knew how I felt about guns. I'd always been a proponent of gun control, but getting shot while eight-and-a-half-months pregnant had pretty well sealed my disgust for side arms and their devotees. In the wake of that nightmare, Al had showed up at the hospital with a bouquet of carnations and a little pearl-handled pistol, complete with its own Roma leather lady's gun purse. I'd sent him and his armory packing. Now, here he was, trying once again to convert me into a gun-toting member of the NRA.

It was, however, hard to stay angry when everyone was so superfriendly. I walked into the building under the banner proudly proclaiming it to be the city's largest indoor firearm range and was greeted by a smiling young man in an Oxford-cloth button-down shirt. He complimented me on my Dodgers cap and invited me to wait for Al in the lounge, a friendly little room with a bank of vinyl chairs and a gurgling coffeemaker. A pleasant, middle-aged woman with gray blue hair molded into perfect curls pressed a flyer about "Ladies' Night" at the range into my hands and complimented me on my new red jeans. Everyone there seemed to like how I dressed.

I willed myself to avoid the plate of doughnuts and home-made cookies sitting invitingly next to the coffee machine and finally compromised by taking just half of a honey-glazed. I was licking my fingers after finishing the second half (it seemed rude to leave a half-eaten doughnut just sitting there on the plate) and leafing through a brochure urging me to practice my shotgun skills with some AA Flyer Clay Targets when Al finally showed up.

"Why are we meeting here?" I asked.

He dumped the black nylon duffel bag he was carrying over his shoulder onto one of the vinyl chairs.

"I needed to get some target practice in. What do you have for me?"

I spent about fifteen minutes describing the various facts about a murderer's history that the California courts consider relevant in determining whether he should be executed for his crimes. I'd printed out a good law review article on the subject. Al was grateful both for the article and for the information.

"You see," he said, "this is why you should go into business with me. You figure out the legal stuff, and I do the legwork. We'd be a good team."

"*You* do the legwork? Please. When I was at the federal defender's office, I didn't just sit behind a desk. You and I went out in the field together. Or have you gotten too senile to remember our days interviewing methamphetamine addicts and robbery witnesses?"

"Prove it," he said with a smile.

"Prove what?"

"Prove that you're capable of doing something other than prancing around a courtroom. Come shoot with me."

I gave a disgusted snort. "How would that prove *anything?* I don't have to shoot a gun to show that I can investigate a crime. I didn't carry a gun when I tracked down my baby-sitter after she'd disappeared. I didn't carry a gun when I confronted Abigail Hathaway's murderer."

"Yeah, well, maybe if you had been the one carrying a weapon, you wouldn't have been the one bleeding on the floor."

I was about to launch into a speech about how people who own guns are more likely to be shot with their own weapons than they are to shoot anyone else but bit back the words. Al and I had had this fight too many times before.

"Speaking of investigations, have you found out anything new about your trainer?" Al asked. Clearly he also wanted to preempt our all-too-familiar debate.

I gave him a quick synopsis of the confusing search for Bobby's birth parents.

"I'm beginning to wonder if any of this is even related to his death," I said.

Al shrugged his shoulders and said, "My operating assumption has always been that there are no coincidences. Here this guy shoots himself—"

"Or someone shoots him," I interrupted. "Don't forget the Palm Pilot."

"You're really stuck on that, aren't you?"

"I just don't think someone would order a Palm Pilot on-line and then kill himself before it even has a chance to arrive. And, anyway, Bobby just wasn't a depressed kind of guy."

"Okay, either he shoots himself, or someone shoots him, and he just so happens to have recently found out that he's adopted and is looking for his biological parents. It's got to be linked."

"Because there are no such things as coincidences."

"Exactly."

"It's a good theory. It's certainly the one I've been operating on. There's just one problem with it."

"What?"

"There *are* such things as coincidences. They happen all the time."

He shrugged again.

"Hey, you wouldn't consider doing me the usual favor and calling one of your LAPD buddies to check on the status of the case, would you?" I asked.

"Sure, if you do one other thing for me."

"Anything!"

"Come shoot with me."

I rolled my eyes. "No."

"Listen to me for a minute. I know you're opposed to the idea of people carrying guns, but don't you think your arguments might carry a little more weight if you actually knew what you were talking about? Try it. Take a couple of practice shots. You might find out that you like it."

"I won't like it."

"How do you know, until you try?"

So I did.

And I did. Like it, that is.

Fourteen

DESPITE the bright yellow sign informing us that the range was equipped to handle semiautomatic pistols, rifles, and even fully automatic machine guns, and that they would happily rent those weapons out to us if we didn't bring our own, Al gave me a small handgun to shoot with. It was black, and heavy, and the handle warmed up quickly in my sweating palm.

He stood behind me in the little booth and watched as I held out the gun with a shaking arm, took aim at a pink silhouette on a sliding metal rack, and jerked the trigger back. Nothing happened.

"Safety's on," Al said.

"What?" I asked, lifting up my ear guards.

"Safety." He took the gun from me and disengaged the

safety with a practiced thumb. "Squeeze the trigger. Don't jerk."

"What?" I had the ear guards back in place.

"Squeeze. Gently," he said once I'd freed up an ear.

"Oh. Okay. Like a camera. Squeeze." I aimed as best I could and squeezed. The gun went off with a muffled bang, and my arm jerked. I squinted at the target. To my utter astonishment, there was a mark on the lower left-hand side of the target. I'd hit it.

"Wow!" I said. "I must be a natural. Check that out."

"Not bad. Try again."

The next time, however, I was anticipating the recoil. I couldn't help but flinch as I pulled the trigger. I looked up at the target. It had suffered no further damage.

I raised my eyebrows at Al and said, "Gee, you're right. It is too bad I didn't have a gun when I was investigating the Hathaway murder. I could have fired at her killer and missed. That would have been both smart and effective, don't you think?"

My sarcasm was lost on Al. He motioned at me, and I lifted up the ear guards. "Why don't you try keeping your eyes open," he said.

That's when I started having fun. The next time, I opened my eyes, lined up the target in my sights, and squeezed the trigger, reminding myself not to flinch in anticipation of the recoil. I blasted a hole at the bottom of the target, just where a man might find it most painful.

After that, I couldn't be stopped. I fired single rounds, taking careful aim. That soon got boring, and I experimented with emptying my gun into the target as quickly as I could. I turned down Al's offer of his shotgun and instead tried out his M-9 semiautomatic pistol. The thing weighed at least two pounds, and it took me a while to figure out how to keep the nose up and my arm steady. Once I had that down, however, it was a little distressing how much fun I had firing off the fifteen rounds.

After a couple of hours, Al and I repaired to an early lunch of doughnuts and coffee.

"I told you I'd make a convert out of you," he said.

I snorted the coffee out of my nose. Wiping at the brown stain on my white T-shirt, I shook my head. "Al, you really don't get it, do you?"

"What?"

"I'm not surprised that I had fun. I mean, there's a reason millions of adolescent boys spend all their free time and money in arcades playing Cop-killer or whatever those games are called. Target shooting is *fun.* I don't have a problem with target shooting. If guns were only available at shooting ranges, I'd be perfectly happy. It's the fact that any certified lunatic can buy an assault rifle and mow down a preschool class that bugs me. Or the fact that every single one of my gang-banger clients has an arsenal the size of a National Guard unit. By the way, their guns are legally purchased as often as not. It's the *availability* of a deadly toy that I find so problematic, not that people have fun playing with them."

He opened his mouth, but I didn't give him time to interrupt. "And don't you dare offer to give me one for my own protection. I have two kids, one of whom is a gun nut.

I'm not bringing a gun into my house," I said.

I recognized the look that crossed over his face. His eyes held a very definite "Now's the time to teach them gun safety" kind of gleam. But, to my relief, he snapped his mouth shut in a thin line and even, after a moment or two, managed a smile.

"Well, intelligent minds can disagree, I suppose," he said.

"Yup." I nodded.

TRUE to his word, Al used his cell phone to call a couple of his buddies at the LAPD. His old partner was at his desk and put him on hold while he made a call to the Santa Monica Police Department, where Bobby's case was lodged. He was back within minutes. Al nodded and thanked the guy.

"Well?" I said.

"Closed. Cause of death deemed suicide."

"Are they absolutely sure?"

Al shrugged. "Who knows. But they closed the case."

I stared at him for a moment. "Yeah, well, I haven't closed mine," I said.

Fifteen

IN order to get out to meet Al unencumbered by children, I had dropped Ruby off at a friend's for an all-day playdate and left Isaac sitting in our bed watching a *Zaboomafoo* marathon on PBS, a sports bottle of chocolate milk in one hand and a defrosted bagel in the other. Peter hadn't even woken up when I'd rolled him over to make room for his son, and I'd given Isaac strict instructions that if he needed anything, he should kick his father until he gained consciousness. Despite the fact that I'd left the house almost three hours before, neither of the men in my life had budged.

Isaac's eyes were glazed over from watching three hours of the Kratt brothers engaging in their particular brand of frenzied animal-watching—sort of like Mutual of Omaha's *Wild Kingdom* but on speed and with better jokes.

"Hi Mama. I'm a lemur," my son told me when I walked

in the room. He'd eaten his bagel and used his chocolate milk to paint his face with a couple of lemurish black stripes.

"So you are. Is Daddy still asleep?"

"Yeah."

"Did he wake up at all?"

"Yeah, but he didn't want to watch TV, so he put the pillow over his head."

It was nice to know I wasn't the only neglectful parent in the house. I scooped Isaac out of bed, set him gently on the floor, and whipped the covers off my insentient husband with a shriek that wouldn't have embarrassed a banshee. He leapt about sixteen feet in the air.

"Good morning, darling," I purred.

He growled at me and stomped off to the shower. I followed him into the bathroom and leaned against the cold tile wall.

"I'm going to need you to spend some more of that fabulous quality time with Isaac today," I shouted over the sound of the water.

He grunted.

I didn't call Susan before driving over to her house. I figured there was a good chance I'd catch her at home on a Sunday afternoon, and I didn't want to give her the chance to avoid me. The sense of righteous indignation that I'd felt after talking to Reuben Nadelman had abated somewhat, but I was still eager to confront her with what I knew. If I caught her unawares, she was less likely to be able to come up with another in the series of half-truths and outright lies with which she had already tried to confuse me.

I pulled up the long driveway, wondering how once again mine were the only tire tracks in the combed gravel. Did the Sullivan family drive hovercraft? Salud obviously had Sundays off, because a handsome older man with pale, blondish gray hair and a weather-beaten face answered the door. He looked like a man who spent a lot of time outside, even if just on the golf course. He was wiry and thin, but his height gave him the impression of bulk.

"Yes? Can I help you?" he asked.

"Hello, I'm Juliet Applebaum. I'm a . . . a friend of Susan's. Is she in?"

He sized me up for a minute, not having missed the stumble my voice made over the word *friend*. I got the feeling that very little got by this man.

"Please come in." He led me through the now-familiar entranceway and back into a large, sunny kitchen. Half of the room was a fairly unremarkable kitchen with the usual cabinetry and appliances. The other half was graced with an impressive oversized stone fireplace, in front of which stood a large, round oak table. The table was set with pretty blue and white dishes and contained the remains of what had obviously been an elaborate brunch. There was a half-eaten platter of berries carefully arranged by color, and a wicker basket with a bright blue gingham ribbon and a few crumbly muffins and croissants nestled in a matching napkin. Susan sat flanked by two handsome, blond men in their mid- to late twenties. I recognized one as the young man who had pushed Isaac on the swing. The other was clearly his older brother. The two looked remarkably alike, and they both resembled Bobby to an uncanny degree. He, too, had possessed those same handsome, innocuous features and surfer-boy, blond hair.

A pregnant woman in a pale pink sweater that precisely matched her lipstick, her dark hair held back by a thick velvet band, also sat at the table. Near the fireplace, in a low armchair, sat an elderly woman dressed in a severe navy suit tied at the neck with a floppy white bow. Her long, wrinkled earlobes were weighed down by huge, yellowish diamonds that looked like they could use a cleaning, and she was speaking as I came into the room.

"I wish you'd joined Patrick and me at Mass this morning, Susan. Father Fitzgerald gave a lovely sermon. Truly inspiring. It's been so long since you've heard him speak. When was the last time you went to church, dear?"

Everyone looked up as I walked into the room. When Susan saw me, her face froze, and red splotches began to appear under the freckles on her cheeks and neck. Both young men glanced at her. They wore identical looks of concern.

"Hello, Susan. I was just passing by and hoped we might have a word," I said, the bright tone of my voice ringing falsely in my ears and, I'm sure, in theirs.

"Yes. Yes of course," she said, rising suddenly. "Let's talk in the garden."

"Susan," the older woman said. "Hadn't you best introduce your friend to us? Or am I the only person who hasn't had the pleasure?"

"Oh, of course. Of course," Susan mumbled awkwardly. "Juliet, this is my mother-in-law, Mary-Margaret Sullivan. Marmie, my . . . friend Juliet." Her voice tripped over the word, as mine had earlier. "Juliet, these are my sons P. J.," she pointed to the older young man who was a bit stockier than his brother. "And you met Matthew the other day. P. J.'s wife Charlotte. And of course my husband Patrick."

I smiled politely and shook hands all around. The boys' handshakes were firm, like their father's, but Susan's mother-in-law's palm lay like a bundle of dry sticks in my own.

"We'll be outside," Susan said, motioning me to a set of French doors behind the table.

"Are you all right, Mom?" Matthew asked, his brow wrinkled with concern.

"Your mother's fine," his father said, and the young man blushed and stared down at his plate of half-eaten, congealing quiche.

"It's nothing, honey," Susan said soothingly. "Juliet and I are just trying to work out some problems with the library benefit. Lots of last-minute crises, as usual." The woman sure was a fluid liar. But, then, she'd had a lot of practice. She put a hand on my arm and pushed me out through the door. Her nails dug through my shirtsleeve, and I had to work hard to keep from wincing.

"What are you doing here?" she asked, once the door had closed behind us. "I've told you all about Bobby. Why can't you just leave me alone?" She sat down heavily in one of the Adirondack chairs, and I made myself comfortable in the other.

"Have you?"

"Have I what?"

"Have you told me all about Bobby?"

"What do you mean? I've told you everything I know."

"I went to visit Reuben Nadelman yesterday."

She looked at me sharply, and I could see that she was desperate to know more. She didn't speak for a moment and then, in a small voice, said, "How is he? Is he married? Does he have other children?"

"He's married. And he has one son. At least, he has a son whom he considers his. The boy is not his biological child, however."

"What do you mean?" Susan began twisting the ring around her finger.

"Reuben is infertile. His son was conceived through artificial insemination of donor sperm."

She shook her head. "That's just not possible. If he's infertile now, he wasn't twenty-eight years ago. He was certainly fertile enough to get me pregnant."

"Susan, Reuben Nadelman is not a Tay-Sachs carrier. If he is Bobby's father, then Bobby would have had to inherit the gene from you."

"But, I'm *not* a Tay-Sachs carrier. I told you. I'm not Jewish, and anyway, I took that test, and it came out negative."

I leaned forward in my chair, giving Susan a look that I hoped was piercing. "Well, then you know what this means," I said.

"What? What does it mean?"

"If Bobby didn't inherit the gene from you, then he must

have inherited it from his father. And if you don't have it, and neither does Reuben Nadelman, then Reuben can't be Bobby's father. So who is, Susan? Who is Bobby Katz's father?"

Something flickered across her face, but I couldn't tell what. "There is some mistake. Either Bobby's test was wrong, or Reuben's test was wrong. I know that Reuben got me pregnant."

"Couldn't it have been someone else?" I asked.

"No!" her voice was sharp and angry. "I don't want to talk to you anymore," she said. "I'm finished talking about this. I have nothing more to say about Bobby or anything else. I want you to leave. You can walk around the house to the front. You know the way." And with that, she rose to her feet and walked unsteadily into the house, closing the French doors firmly behind her.

Sixteen

As I drove down Sunset Boulevard, I puzzled over what Susan had told me. None of this made any sense. Who was Bobby Katz's real father? Had Susan had another lover, a lover of whom she was so ashamed that she refused to talk about him?

It didn't seem possible that there was someone worse in Susan's mind than Reuben Nadelman. She'd been so worried about not foisting a Jewish child off on an unsuspecting Catholic family that she'd gone to great pains to make sure she gave him to a Jewish family. Yet she'd admitted to me that she'd had an affair with Reuben. What could be that much worse than a Jewish lover in her eyes? *Who* could be worse? I tried to imagine what person would be so unacceptable that Susan Sullivan would pretend to have had a child by a Jew rather than admit to an affair with him. A convicted felon? A relative? Her father? Her father-in-law?

That thought made me slam on the brakes. A silver sports car swerved quickly around me. I inhaled sharply as it bulleted in front of me. Thank God for the other driver's reflexes. I was going to have to figure out a way to cut down on the emotive driving if I wanted to see out my fourth decade. I thought again about the Faye Dunaway-in-*Chinatown* scenario I had shocked myself by imagining. It just didn't make sense, however. Neither Susan's father nor her father-in-law were likely to be Bobby's father. Unless Susan was lying about her genetic test, the man who had contributed his little bundle of chromosomes to Bobby's creation had been a Tay-Sachs carrier. While it was theoretically possible that one of those men carried the gene, it was a ridiculously long shot. And if there's one thing I learned in all my years of investigating and trying cases, it was the logical principle of Occam's razor. The simplest and most obvious explanation is most often the true one.

None of this got me any closer to discovering what had happened to Bobby. Had he or had he not committed suicide? If he had, was his despondency related to his adoption and what he'd found out about his birth parents, or was there some other motivation for it altogether? I couldn't seem to accept the suicide theory; it didn't make sense, given everything I knew about Bobby. However, if it wasn't suicide, then it was murder. The fact that Bobby had been found with the weapon ruled out a random killing, to my mind. None of the many drive-by shooters and carjackers I'd come across in my public defender days left their weapons behind.

Professional criminals, and by that I mean those who engage in illegal behavior for profit, value their weapons. They're attached to them. More importantly, the guns cost money. The last thing these guys want to do is throw money away. If Bobby's death were the result of a random act of violence, the killer wouldn't have left the gun behind.

No, if Bobby was murdered, he was murdered by someone he knew, and that person had done his or her best to make the crime look like suicide. As Al has told me time and time again, look to the family. More often than not, the only people who hate us enough to kill us are those who are supposed to love us the most. The question was, which of Bobby's families? He had so many.

My cell phone rang. The caller ID screen was flashing "Home."

"Hi, Peter," I said. "How are you guys doing?"

"We're good. We just built a model Native American village out of Lego blocks."

"What a good dad you are. And so PC."

"Yeah, whatever. Listen, I'll make you a deal."

"What?"

"I'll give you the whole rest of the afternoon on your own if you do kid duty tonight so I can catch a movie with a couple of the guys."

A few more hours of freedom! "Sure, no problem," I said, doing my best to convey the false impression that I was doing him a favor. "I'll be home before dinner."

"Take your time."

In the background I heard banging and shrieking. "What's that?" I asked.

"Isaac's bringing in the cavalry to attack the village. I'd better go help Ruby rescue the women and children."

I hit the End button and tapped the steering wheel. *Look to the family,* I thought to myself. Bobbie and Betsy weren't married, but they were about to be. Maybe I needed to look a little more closely at the person on whose behalf I was supposedly investigating this case. I made a quick right onto Melrose Avenue and headed over to Hollywood.

I found Betsy still sober, to my great relief, and looking much better than when I'd seen her last. She'd finally gotten up the energy to wear something other than sweats. She had on a pair of black flared jeans with neon green roses embroidered down one leg, and a green Lycra top that clung tightly to her body, outlining her breasts and leaving bare the little roll at her midriff. She had a small gold hoop in her bellybutton. Her hair was freshly cut, and she'd put on lipstick. In fact, she looked a heck of a lot better than I did.

"Roy, this is Juliet Applebaum, the client of Bobby's who's been trying to track down what was going on with him before he died. Juliet, this is my friend Roy West."

I shook the hand of the small man who had been sitting with Betsy. He looked about forty, with graying hair cropped close to his head and gold grommets punched into both earlobes. A third bit of gold poked through one of his eyebrows. He looked too old for his metal decorations, and he smelled strongly of cigarette smoke. He took a great swig from the oversized plastic L.A. Dodgers cup he held in his hand and belched softly. There was a bottle of Diet Coke on the coffee table. I was willing to bet the farm that Roy was a friend from AA. The smoking and copious caffeine consumption gave him away.

Betsy hadn't shown much ability to keep on the wagon in the absence of Bobby's positive influence. I was glad to see that she had fallen back in with the AA circle. Hopefully, their support would give her the strength she needed to stay straight.

I told Betsy that I hadn't found out much more about Bobby's birth family, and in fact was even more confused than ever before. I paused, waiting for her response. I didn't know exactly what I was looking for or what I hoped she would tell me. Mostly, I just wanted to get a better sense of her. Could she have had something to do with her fiancé's death?

"Are you sure Bobby's Tay-Sachs test was accurate?" I asked.

She shrugged. "I guess so. I mean, we had it done at UCLA. I can't imagine they would screw it up."

I couldn't either. "Do you think I could take another look through Bobby's things?"

"What are you looking for?"

"I don't really know." I shrugged. "I guess I'm just on a fishing expedition."

"Well, you'll have to fish somewhere else," Roy interrupted.

"Excuse me?" I asked.

"The Katzes came over here and cleaned Betsy out. They

took all of Bobby's files, his office furniture, even his books. It was all we could do to keep their hands off the living room furniture."

"Roy said it was mine, and he knew, because he helped me move it in from my old apartment." She smiled at him.

He preened. "I was happy to do it. Lying to those creeps is a good deed."

I looked from one of them to the other. It dawned on me that they might be either sleeping together or inching toward it. A new boyfriend would explain Betsy's transformation from depressed widow to Lycra-clad babe. Or was he new? Was it possible that she'd been seeing him even before Bobby died?

I made small talk for a little while, watching them closely. There definitely seemed to be some kind of chemistry between the two. Betsy brushed against Roy's arm as she picked up his cup to refill it. He put an arm around her shoulder when she mentioned Bobby. It was a comforting gesture, but it seemed more intimate than simply supportive.

"Are you going to keep investigating?" Betsy asked me.

"I don't know what more I can do," I said. "I might ask Bobby's parents if they'll let me see his papers. Maybe they'll let me look through his hard drive again. I can't imagine that I'll find anything, though. It's really a puzzle."

Betsy nodded. "I've been running through this over and over in my mind, and I just can't think of any reason for Bobby to have killed himself. I know I was kind of wrapped up in my own problems, but I still think I would have noticed if Bobby had been depressed. He just wasn't like that. He didn't get blue. If he was bumming, he'd just go work out."

I agreed with this assessment. I certainly didn't know Bobby as well as she did, but in all our time together, he'd never been anything but upbeat. Even when Betsy had gotten into trouble, Bobby had retained his positive outlook. He'd been convinced that it was just a matter of working harder to help her with her recovery.

"Bobby didn't kill himself," Betsy said firmly.

"I hate to say this, but maybe it was a drug deal gone bad," Roy said.

"Roy! Bobby would never have done that!" Betsy sounded outraged.

"You can't know that, Betsy. Every one of us is just one step away from using. Maybe Bobby took that step. Maybe he arranged to meet some guy out by the beach and got robbed instead."

The thought had occurred to me right after Bobby's death, but I had dismissed it. Bobby had been the poster child for the recovery movement. It just didn't seem possible for him to have fallen off the wagon. Moreover, Bobby was acutely conscious of the health consequences of using. Methamphetamine had become toxic to his body. It didn't make sense that a man devoted to maximizing his physical performance would risk so much. Perhaps, however, I'd been too hasty in casting this drug-deal scenario aside.

"I know it doesn't seem possible, but maybe Roy has a point," I said. "Think back to Bobby's behavior leading up to the day he died. Was he acting strangely in any way? Did he disappear for periods of time?"

"Juliet, I think I would know if he were using. I mean, for God's sake, the warning signs are, like, tattooed on my forehead. He wasn't."

"But wasn't he being unusually secretive? He kept the adoption thing from you. Isn't it at least possible that he kept his drug use from you as well?"

I knew I was cross-examining her. Peter is forever complaining about this habit of mine. Once you learn courtroom techniques, however, it's difficult to abandon them for the niceties of acceptable conversation. For one thing, they are remarkably effective. There's nothing like an insistent barrage of questions for eliciting a response.

Betsy bit her lip. "He did lie to me for months about the adoption. But I would know if he used. Wouldn't I?" she said, plaintively.

I just shrugged my shoulders.

We sat quietly for a little while, and I debated whether or not I should ask Betsy about Candace. That woman was in love with Bobby. Maybe she'd killed him out of frustrated desire. When I brought up her name to Betsy, she shook her head. "No, he didn't say anything. I mean, how could he? He never told me he was adopted, so how could he tell me about meeting some woman on an Internet adoption web site?"

I fumbled around for more to ask Betsy but finally gave up. It gave me pause that Betsy had argued against the possibility of Bobby having killed himself. If she had done it, wouldn't she be more inclined to support the suicide hypothesis? I hadn't learned much in my visit, but neither had my concerns been assuaged. For the time being, I wasn't going to dismiss the possibility that Betsy had had something to do with Bobby's death.

Seventeen

I swore under my breath as I stood looking at the smashed window of Peter's car. Peter's lovingly tended, vintage 2002. The one I'd insisted on driving. The one I'd parked in front of Betsy's apartment, in a part of Hollywood that verged on the seedy.

The front passenger window was shattered, bits of glass littering the ground and the bucket seat. I glanced in the window and was relieved to see that the radio was still there. For once I'd actually remembered to take my purse with me, so that was safe as well. The fact that it seemed to be an act of vandalism rather than theft gave me little comfort, and I stomped around the car to the driver's side. My breath caught in my throat and my stomach lurched when I saw the words scratched into the side of the car. Someone had

written "MIND YOUR OWN BUSINESS," in jagged cap-
ital letters.

The words extended along both driver's-side doors and
were carved with such force that the orange paint had peeled
up around the scratches. I looked quickly up and down the
street. At the end of the block, I saw a two boys playing
around with a broken scooter. They were trying to get up
some speed while balancing on the scooter's remaining
wheel.

"Hey!" I called out to them.

They looked up at me and then continued with their
game.

"Hey!" I said again and walked quickly up the block.
They appeared to be brothers; one was about seven years old,
and the other looked no more than five. They had dark skin
and close-shaved heads, and the older boy wore a gold cross
dangling from a hoop in one ear.

"Did you see anyone near that orange car back there?" I
asked.

The older boy shrugged his shoulders, and the younger
boy giggled.

"Did you?" I asked again.

"Maybe," the older boy said. "How much you pay me to
tell you?"

I crouched down next to him and said, in my best
mommy voice, "Listen young man, if you don't tell me who
scratched up my car, I'm going to find your mother. I bet
she'll make you talk."

He clicked his tongue and said, "I don't know nothin'
'bout your car."

"Fredo, that rich dude was hangin' out by the orange car, remember?" the younger brother said.

"You shut up," the older boy whacked his brother on the top of his head.

"Hey!" I grabbed the older boy's arm. "No hitting."

"Yeah, Fredo! No hitting," the little boy said, his lip trembling.

"Fredo, tell me what happened to my car," I said.

The boy rolled his eyes. "Fine. Whatever. This phat car pulled up next to yours, and this dude got out. That's all we know. Honest. I don't know what he did or nothing. He was just, like, walking around your car."

"Did you see him break the window?"

The little boys shook their heads.

"Do you know what kind of car he was driving?"

"No. It was phat."

"Fat?"

The little boys rolled their eyes at my ignorance. "You know, cool. Awesome. Like a racing car," Fredo said.

"What color was the racing car?"

"Metal," said the younger boy.

PETER'S face turned a mottled red when I told him what had happened. He rushed out to his beloved car and knelt down next to the driver's-side door. He ran his fingers along the scratches, swearing quietly under his breath.

"I'm so sorry, honey. Really," I said.

"Who did this?" he asked, rising to his feet.

I told him what the two boys had told me. "I'm figuring that by racing car they meant sports car. That's what Isaac calls them, doesn't he?" Among our son's many obsessions was one with the automobile. While Hondas were his inexplicable favorite—he called them Wandas and lovingly stroked each one we passed (it made for slow going on walks)—he was also enamored of anything he could call a racing car. For some mysterious reason, this included both sports cars and taxicabs.

Peter swore again.

"I'm sorry, Peter. Really I am."

"It's not the car that I'm upset about. I mean, yeah, I'm upset about the car. I can't even imagine what it's going to cost to fix this. The scratches go all the way through to the metal. But that's not what I'm worried about."

"I know," I said.

We went back in the house. I called the police department, and while I waited on hold to file a report, the two of us ran through the various people involved in the case, trying to come up with a possible suspect. The problem was that the only person whom I could even remotely imagine doing something like that was the only one I could be sure hadn't been involved. Betsy had been in the room with me the whole time I'd been parked in front of her house. That left the members of Bobby's birth and adoptive families, none of whom seemed a particularly likely candidate for such a brutally juvenile warning. And then there was Candace.

Finally, after I'd waited close to a quarter of an hour on hold, a police officer picked up the line. I told her what had happened and where I'd been parked. Then, I said, "I think this might have something to do with the death of a friend of mine."

The officer, who had seemed up until then utterly bored with the details of yet another act of destruction of property, perked up. "Excuse me?" she asked.

"My friend, Bobby Katz, was found dead in his car a couple of weeks ago. It appeared to be a suicide, and I understand that the Santa Monica Police Department has closed the case. However, I think that someone might have been trying to warn me off any further investigation."

"Are you a private investigator, ma'am?" The cop's voice was frosty.

"No. No, I'm not. I'm a friend of the deceased. I was simply trying to help his fiancée determine what happened to him. Perhaps you can refer this to the detectives assigned to the case."

"Ma'am, there won't be any detectives assigned to a suicide if the case is closed. However, I'm more than happy to pass this information along to someone in the Santa Monica PD."

I was getting the brush-off. "Officer, listen. If Bobby was murdered, then it's very possible that I just got a warning from his killer. I'm concerned. With reason, I think."

"You said your friend committed suicide."

"No, I said that the case had been *ruled* a suicide. There's a difference." I knew I was coming off high-handed, but I was scared, and she was making me angry.

"As I said, ma'am, I'll pass this along. This is your police report number for insurance purposes." She mumbled a string of numbers and then she hung up the phone.

"Well?" Peter asked. He was sitting at the table, holding Isaac on his lap. Isaac was sucking on a tube of yogurt and had a trail of fluorescent pink down the front of his shirt. I swabbed at the stain with a paper towel.

"Well?" my husband repeated.

"I don't think they're going to do anything."

"Juliet, I'm worried about this."

"I know. I am, too."

"What are you going to do?"

"I don't know. Wait to hear from the police, I guess."

"I won't hold my breath." He kissed the top of Isaac's head. For a split second, I wished I'd taken Al up on his offer. I imagined confronting this fear with a loaded revolver. I couldn't help but wonder if I'd feel safer.

"I'm going to call Bobby's parents," I said.

"Which ones?"

"The Katzes. Maybe they'll let me take another look at Bobby's things. If the cops aren't going to do anything, I'm going to have to track down whoever is responsible myself."

Peter compressed his lips in a thin line but didn't say anything. He picked up Isaac and carried him out to the playroom, where Ruby was busy building a dollhouse out of blocks. I couldn't tell whether he was angry with me for continuing my investigation or whether he understood that it was my only option. I couldn't tell, and I didn't try to find out.

I dug Bobby's parents' phone number out of my purse

and picked up the phone. His father answered. Before I could make my request, he said, "Ms. Applebaum, we all appreciate that you are trying to help. However, I must insist that you refrain from continuing in these efforts. It's a violation of Bobby's privacy. And of ours."

I had been expecting something like this. "I understand that you might feel that way, Dr. Katz. But Betsy isn't convinced that Bobby committed suicide. It's possible that I'll be able to uncover enough information to convince the police to reopen the case."

"Betsy is a deluded and manipulative drug addict, who seems to have sucked you into her fantasy or beguiled you into going along with her plans, whatever those may be. What she thinks about Bobby is utterly irrelevant. The police, the coroner, the medical examiner, all agree that Bobby killed himself. Your pursuit of intimate details of his life is not only unhelpful but destructive." The doctor's voice was cold and harsh, but I wasn't giving up. Someone had struck out at me, had threatened me. It was personal now. I was too angry and too scared to back off.

"I'm terribly sorry to have offended you, Dr. Katz. But I have reason to believe not only that Bobby was murdered, but that the murderer is trying to scare me off the investigation." I told him about the warning on my car.

He snorted derisively. "I haven't any idea who did that to your car, Ms. Applebaum. Moreover, it's ludicrous for you to imagine that it had anything to do with Bobby's death. You parked in a lousy neighborhood. Be more careful next time." And with that, he hung up on me.

My tenacity in the face of opposition is either my best or worst quality, depending on whom you ask. When I was a child, it was a source of intense frustration to my poor parents, who took a remarkably long time figuring out that the best way to get me to do something was to tell me not to. Peter has proved to be a better manipulator and generally avoids being on the wrong side of my intransigence. In fact, because he's not a particularly obstinate person himself, he has always relished having, as he says, a pit bull in his corner. I myself grew somewhat less comfortable with this particular side of my personality when I began seeing it reflected back at me in Ruby's face. My daughter makes me look positively irresolute; she doesn't have a pliable bone in her body. She came out of me with her little fists balled and raised and has been bashing her way through the world ever since.

I was debating the merits of driving out to Thousand Oaks and blustering into the Katzes' home when the phone rang. It took me a moment to figure out that the whispering voice on the other end of the line belonged to Bobby's sister, Michelle.

"I'm so sorry about my dad, Juliet. I just want you to know that not all of us think that way."

"What way?" I asked.

"Not all of us think that Bobby killed himself. I mean, I don't. He couldn't have. And I really appreciate what you've been doing. It's *my* fault my dad is all up in arms about this."

"Your fault?"

"Yes," she said apologetically. "I didn't mean to get them upset or to get you in trouble." That was a funny phrase for a grown woman to use. "But when my mother and David told us about your investigation, I tried to convince my parents to let you go forward. I'm convinced that there is more to this than the police think."

"Michelle, why are we whispering?"

"Oh, I'm sorry." I could almost hear her blushing. "I'm at my parents' house, and I'm on my cell phone. In the bathroom. I didn't want my dad to know that I was calling you."

The Drs. Katz were so formidable that they reduced their grown-up daughter, a woman of significant accomplishment in her own right, to a teenager sneaking a telephone call while pretending to use the toilet.

"There are a few things that I'd really like to talk about, and I can't imagine you'll be able to stay in the bathroom for long. Can you meet me?" I said.

"What? Now?"

"Yes. I mean, it doesn't have to be right now, but it might as well be. Did your father tell you that someone threatened me?" I told Michelle about Peter's car.

"Oh no! That's awful. You must be terrified." That was too strong a word. Nervous? Yes. Scared, even. But the feeling of foreboding inspired by the vandalism of the BMW certainly didn't rise to the level of terror. Or so I tried to convince myself.

"I guess I could meet you," Michelle continued. "I could pretend that I have to go into the office."

It took me a while to convince Peter that I wasn't taking any unnecessary risks by talking to Michelle. He finally agreed that I should go but insisted that he come along, too. And, since we were both going, Ruby and Isaac were necessarily invited along for the ride.

"We'll have dinner at the mall," I said, brightly, as if the prospect of limp egg rolls and gyro platters was an enticement. Actually, for them it probably was.

By the time we arrived, Michelle was already waiting for me at an orange plastic table in the food court.

I sat down opposite her and waved Peter in the direction of the California Pizza Kitchen. "I'll find you guys in about half an hour," I told him. I was about to ask him to get me a couple of slices of pizza but changed my mind. Michelle was one of those tiny little women who can't find enough size twos to flesh out a decent wardrobe. I amended that to a Caesar salad. With the dressing on the side.

Michelle and I watched Peter and the kids wander off. Ruby was skipping ahead, and Isaac was sitting on his father's shoulders.

"You have a lovely family," she said.

"Thanks. Do you have kids?"

She shook her head. "No, not yet. We're thinking about it, but my hours are really crazy. Larry didn't even bat an eyelash when I told him and my parents that I had to go to work tonight. I probably spend more Sunday nights at work than at home."

"That's hard," I said. I certainly wasn't about to feed her

the line about how it was perfectly reasonable to expect to have a demanding career and be an active and involved parent. I'd discovered the folly of that the hard way. But Michelle was at least thirty-five years old, if not older. She didn't have a lot of time to debate the pros and cons of reproduction. No way I was going to tell her that, either.

"Anyway, like I said on the phone, I really do appreciate your trying to help us figure out what happened to Bobby," she said.

If there was anyone who could help me rule out the possibility that Bobby had killed himself, maybe it was this woman, who loved him so much and knew him so well. "I'm sure you've gone over this a thousand times in your mind," I said, "but thinking about everything that happened to Bobby right before his death—Betsy's arrest, his discovery that he was adopted—does it seem possible that he could have been depressed enough to commit suicide?"

She shook her head. Tears welled up in her eyes and threatened to spill over. "I just don't believe Bobby could have done that. He wasn't like that. I mean, he definitely had a self-destructive side. I guess you know about his methamphetamine problem."

I nodded.

"But he kicked that. Completely. He'd put all that behind him."

"You don't think that what happened with Betsy might have pushed him over the edge?"

"Of course Betsy's relapse made him *sad,* that's only natural. But you should have heard him defend her to my parents. He told them that addiction is a physical and mental disease and lectured them on tolerance and understanding. He was amazing. He stood by her the whole time, and honestly, I don't think he would have abandoned her now, when she's back in treatment and doing so well."

I cringed a bit, remembering Betsy's jag. "What about finding out about the adoption? Could that have depressed him sufficiently?"

Michelle shook her head. "Bobby wasn't depressed or sad about that. I mean, he was furious with our parents for not telling him. But he wasn't upset about being adopted. On the contrary. He seemed really excited about finding his birth mother. You see, our mother is a wonderful woman. She's smart and strong and a real . . . a real . . ." I was tempted to fill her pause with the word *bitch*, but restrained myself. "She's wonderful," Michelle repeated lamely. "But, she's very demanding. And she's not a real affectionate person. Neither is my dad. I think Bobby needed that more than the rest of us did. It's like Lisa, David, and I were kind of hardwired for my parents—we weren't particularly needy children. But Bobby was wired for something else. He always wanted more of a certain kind of attention than my parents could give. And the attention they did give, the way they got involved in our schoolwork, in our grades, well, that didn't usually work out so well for Bobby. He never excelled academically, so the fact that that was the way they showed their interest in him ended up causing him anxiety and stress instead of anything positive."

"It sounds like he didn't really fit your parents' ideal of what a child should be like."

She shook her head. "No, he certainly didn't. After a while, they stopped demanding so much of him; after all, they had the three of us to satisfy them. Don't get me wrong," she said urgently. "They loved Bobby. Really they did. It was just a difficult relationship."

"Why did they adopt him in the first place? I mean, they already had three children. Why did they want another?" I wanted to see if Michelle's answer matched that of her mother's.

"They always planned to have four children—two boys and a two girls. They'd even timed everything perfectly so that their residencies wouldn't be disrupted. But then my mom had to have C-sections with all of us. My birth was particularly hard on her, and the doctors were afraid that if she got pregnant again, she might have a uterine rupture. At first I think my parents accepted that. After all, they did wait eight years before they adopted Bobby. But, finally, I guess they decided that they really had to have their picture-perfect family complete with two of each kind of kid. So they adopted a little baby boy."

"Do you think that Bobby was eager to find his birth parents because he imagined that they might give him the kind of acceptance that your parents never could?"

Michelle looked thoughtful. "I suppose that's possible. I only ever really talked about the adoption with him twice. The first time was right after he found out. David told him, and then the next weekend, he asked Lisa and me to meet him at Mom and Dad's. He told us that he had something important to talk about with the whole family. It was pretty

intense. He sat us all down in the kitchen and told us that
he knew about the adoption. At first my father tried to pretend that he didn't know what Bobby was talking about. I
mean, he'd been pretending for so long.

"But Bobby didn't let my dad get away with it. First, he
tried to get Lisa and me to admit it, but I guess we were
just too freaked out to say anything. I remember Lisa was
leafing through a medical journal of Mom's, and she just sat
there, pretending to read. I don't even know what I was
doing. Probably trying to look invisible."

"What made your father finally admit the truth?"

"Bobby was getting angrier and angrier. I think initially
he was trying to protect David so that my parents wouldn't
know that he was the one who told, but when they kept
insisting that it wasn't true, he told them that David had
told him everything. It was horrible. He just looked at Dad
and said, "Stop lying. For once just stop lying.""

"Your father told him the truth?"

Michelle shook her head. "No, my mother did. She said
that it was true, but that it didn't mean anything. That it
didn't mean they didn't love him. She even hugged him,
which if you knew my mother, you'd know is a huge deal.
She's not a hugger."

"How did Bobby respond?"

"He ended up bursting into tears. I did, too, and I swear
I even saw tear in Mom's eye. Bobby told us that he loved
us, and that he wasn't upset about being adopted. He asked
my parents what they knew about his birth mother, but we
all could see right away that the question really upset them.

From the very beginning, they were absolutely opposed to his finding out anything about her. I think they finally told him that Jewish Family Services would never tell them anything beyond his birth date and the fact that his mother was healthy. I don't know if they know any specific facts, but I'm pretty confident that even if they do, they wouldn't have told Bobby anything else. Mom especially didn't think anything good could come out of looking for his birth mother. She told Bobby that it was obvious that the woman hadn't wanted him, so he should just concentrate on the people who did. Namely, her and Dad. And us, of course."

"How did it all end?"

"I guess we all just told Bobby how much we loved him again, and he told us that he loved us, too. And then we never really talked about it much as a family again."

"But you talked about it with Bobby?"

"Yeah, one other time. He had given me a free training session for my birthday, so I came down to his gym in Hollywood. He told me that he was looking for his birth mother, and we started imagining what she was like. We figured that she was Jewish, since the adoption had come through Jewish Family Services. Bobby was sure she had been really young, probably a teenager, and that she'd given him up because she wasn't able to care for him. He was confident that she'd be interested in meeting him, particularly since so much time had passed, and he obviously wasn't after anything from her. He said that it was even possible that she was looking for him, too."

"Did he ever tell you that he found her?"

"No, but he did, didn't he?"

I wondered for a moment whether I should tell Michelle what I knew. I decided to; she was Bobby's sister. She loved him. She had a right to know. "Yes, he did," I said.

"And was she a teenager? I mean, when she gave him up?"

"No, she was young, in her midtwenties, but she was married. Her husband was off fighting in Vietnam, and she had an affair."

Michelle nodded. "That makes sense, I guess. Was she Jewish?"

"No, Catholic."

"Then why did she go through a Jewish adoption agency? And how did Bobby get Tay-Sachs? Was the father Jewish?"

"He must have been. It's a little confusing." I told her about Reuben Nadelman.

"But if he isn't a Tay-Sachs carrier, and neither is she, then there's something wrong. He can't be the father."

"Right."

"So who is?"

"That's one of the things I've been trying to figure out."

"Did she have an affair with anyone else?"

"Not that she's told me about. But I suppose she must have."

"That person would have to be the Tay-Sachs carrier, then. You know, his father doesn't *have* to be Jewish. The disease is not limited to Jews, it's just more prevalent in the Ashkenazic Jewish population."

"I know. It also appears in French Canadians and Cajuns."

"And in the general population, too," she said, "it's just very, very rare."

We sat quietly for a moment. Then Michelle said, "Was Bobby's birth mother glad when he found her? Was she happy to see him?"

I shook my head. "No. She wasn't. She's still married to the same man and has two kids. I think she was terrified her family would find out about Bobby."

Michelle buried her face in her hands. "Oh, God. Poor Bobby. How awful. How awful to find your mother and have her reject you."

I put my hand on hers to soften what I was about to say. "Is it possible that being rejected by his birth mother, especially given the difficult relationship he had with your parents, might have made him so depressed he would consider taking his own life?"

Her shoulders shook with sobs. "I don't know. Maybe. Oh, poor Bobby. Poor, poor Bobby."

"Michelle," I said, "Can you think of anyone who might have wanted to hurt Bobby? Someone who might have a grudge against him?"

She shook her head. "Absolutely not. You know Bobby. He was the most easygoing guy in the world. He would never hurt anybody, and nobody would want to hurt him."

"What about when he was using drugs? Did he make any enemies that you know of?" It's hard to get through life as a drug addict without pissing off a few people.

"No. Honestly. The only person he hurt was himself."

"Was he ever in any trouble with dealers? Was there ever a time when he couldn't pay for his drugs? When he owed money to people?"

She shook her head. "I don't know. I don't really know anything about his life back then. He did a good job of hiding all that from us. Even when he was at his worst, he tried to protect us from knowing the truth. None of us even realized that there was anything wrong until he checked himself into rehab."

I paused for a moment, wondering how she'd respond to my next question. "I have to ask this. Do you think that anyone in your family might have any reason to harm Bobby?"

Her face paled. "No. Absolutely not. We loved Bobby. Maybe we didn't do that good of a job of showing it, but we loved him. None of us would have had hurt him. I know that."

I hoped, for her sake, that she was right.

Eighteen

BOTH kids fell asleep in the backseat on the way home from the mall. Peter carried Ruby out of the car, and I hoisted Isaac onto my shoulder and staggered in behind him. It's amazing how heavy a sleeping toddler is. Shushing each other, we tiptoed through the dark house and gently laid the kids in their beds. I considered wiping the dried ketchup off their faces but wasn't willing to risk waking them. Peter turned the TV on to his favorite B-movie channel, and I went into the kitchen to make myself a cup of chamomile tea. I could already tell I was going to need some help falling asleep.

While I was waiting for the water to boil, I noticed the light flashing on the answering machine. The first message was from my friend Stacy.

"Listen, girl, you just lucked out in a major way. One of

my colleagues came back from maternity leave. She told me that her feet grew an entire size while she was pregnant. She used to be a five and a half. Like you. Now she's a six and a half. I bought her entire collection of Manolo Blahniks for you. You are the proud owner of nine pair of stunning shoes. And you owe me nine hundred dollars."

I was about to pick up the phone and describe to Stacy exactly what my life was like and how drastically it would have to change to accommodate nine pairs of secondhand stiletto heels, when the answering machine began its next message. An electronically distorted voice warned me, "If you care about what happens to your kid, mind your own business."

In my years dealing with criminals of all sorts, I'd never once been threatened. I'd represented drug dealers who had never been anything but polite. I'd had young men from the Crips and the Bloods treat me with respect and affection. My heroin addict bank robbers never intimidated me. Even the violent offenders had been decent to me, if not to their victims. I'd made prosecutors mad enough to call me all kinds of terrible names, but no one had ever threatened my physical safety. Now, while investigating a supposed suicide, someone was menacing my children.

"What the hell was that?" Peter stood in the doorway, looking grim. Wordlessly, I hit the Replay button and together we listened to the ominous voice.

While the message played, I dialed *69 but was informed by a polite automaton that the call return feature couldn't be used to return our last incoming call.

"Caller ID?" Peter said.

I pressed the button on the back of the receiver. It flashed "Private Caller." I shook my head.

"No luck," I said.

"I'm calling the cops."

"Good idea."

The Los Angeles Police Department proved itself courteous and prompt, if not particularly reassuring, although I'm not sure what Peter and I expected them to do. Two patrol officers came out to the house and walked around the yard. They didn't find anyone, but then we hadn't expected them to. Peter had taped the threatening message off of our digital answering machine with the microcassette recorder he used to take notes for his scripts, and he gave the tape to the officers.

When they left, he turned to me. "What are we going to do?"

I shook my head. "I don't know. Tomorrow morning, I'll call the Santa Monica Police and talk to whoever was assigned to Bobby's case. Maybe they'll reopen it, given all this."

Peter began pacing back and forth. "Should we leave the house? Go to a hotel or something?"

I shook my head. "I don't think so. I mean, the warning was to stop. I'm obviously not going to do anything tonight, so I think we're probably safe."

"Probably? Juliet, do you honestly think that's good enough? The guy threatened our kid. Are you willing to take a chance? I'm sure as hell not."

Something occurred to me. "Why just one?"

"What?"

"Why did he, or she for that matter, threaten just one of the kids? Why not both?"

Peter stared at me like I'd gone mad. "I don't know, and frankly I couldn't care less. Threatening one of them is good enough for me. I'm having a hard time understanding why you aren't more upset about this."

"I *am* upset. I'm scared and I'm angry, but I'm also going to do my damnedest to find out what's going on. Why did the person say 'kid' and not 'kids'?"

Peter sat down in a chair and ran his fingers through his hair. It stood up in agitated spikes all over his head.

Suddenly, I had a brilliant idea. "I'm going to call Al," I said.

"What?"

"Al. I told you he's gone into the independent investigation business. I'm going to hire him to protect us. It probably won't cost any more than going to a hotel, and I know I'd feel safer with him around. Who knows how long it'll be before the police take me seriously, let alone find out who's been doing this? At this point, I'm not even confident I'll be able to convince them to reopen Bobby's case."

AL showed up an hour later, accompanied by a lanky young woman with dark curls held off her face in a ponytail tied with a purple beaded elastic band. She was wearing tight lavender jeans and an LAPD sweatshirt and carried the long duffel Al had brought to the shooting range.

"Never leave weapons in an unattended vehicle," she said by way of greeting and extended her hand to me. I shook it, marveling as I did so at the tiny gemstones imbedded in her purple nails.

"You must be Robyn," I said.

"Yup. Nice to meet you. My dad talks about you all the time. He says he'd like you a lot if you weren't such a bleeding-heart liberal."

Al groaned, and I managed a smile.

I turned to my husband. "Peter, this is Al's daughter. The Olympic biathelete."

"Just an alternate," she said, shaking his hand firmly.

"Peter," Al said. "How would you and the kids like to spend a couple of days with my daughter at our cabin in Big Bear? There's no snow on the ground, and it's too cold to swim, but you guys could do some hiking. We've even got a hot tub."

Peter frowned at me. "Is this really necessary?"

I liked the idea. With Peter and the kids out of town, I could concentrate on tracking down the source of the threatening messages without having to worry about them. This situation had stopped being one I could investigate while lugging Isaac and his stroller around with me. Moreover, Robyn, with her rippling muscles, talonlike fingernails, and bag full of guns, looked to be the ideal bodyguard.

"I think it's a terrific idea," I said. "You were just telling me that we should take these threats seriously. I think you're right. I think we should make sure the kids are safe. And I'm sure they'll be safe with Robyn."

Peter looked over at Robyn, and she nodded resolutely.

"Okay. Fine. Let's all go, then," he said.

"Peter," Al interrupted. "If I were you, I'd feel the same way. I'd want to get my little lady out of harm's way." I bristled at this, but he ignored me. Robyn rolled her eyes and we shared a rueful smile at her prehistoric father's blatant sexism. "But Juliet's the only person who can figure out who's responsible for the threats. She's got to retrace all her steps over the past couple of weeks and try to come up with a list of suspects to take to the police officers investigating the case. But don't you worry. I'll take good care of her for you."

That really was too much. "Thanks, Al, but I can take care of myself. I could definitely use another person to help me investigate, though. If you're volunteering," I said.

Al opened his mouth to retort, but Peter spoke first. "Robyn can take the kids up to Big Bear. I'm staying here with you. What if this guy is serious? No way I'm letting you be here by yourself."

I kissed him on the cheek. "That's so sweet, honey, and I really do appreciate it. But Ruby and Isaac don't know Robyn. We can't just send them off with someone they've never met. Plus, I don't think Robyn signed on for baby-sitting duties."

The young woman shook her head. "There's not a lot I can't handle, but I think a couple of little kids might be beyond me."

I said, "One of us has to go with them, and like Al said, if we're going to figure out who is responsible, I've got to stay here."

We could all see Peter struggling with himself. It has always amazed me how even men who've grown up believing that women are their equals and are competent and strong enough to protect themselves, even men who would call themselves feminists, have a ribbon of machismo running through their personalities. Peter and I certainly have a marriage of equals. Not even the fact that he was currently the sole wage earner had changed that. Nonetheless, when faced with the possibility of peril for his woman, I could see my white knight aching to pick up his lance and head off to battle. Except he knew as well as I did that somebody had to take care of the kids.

The look of resignation in my husband's face inspired me to give him another kiss on the cheek. His pride wounded by the indignity of having to run out of town, he shook me off. I turned to Robyn.

"It's late. Do you want to wait until morning before heading up to Big Bear? You can take the guest room, and I can make up the couch for you, Al," I said.

"You know, I think I'd rather go now. I don't want to try to drive through morning rush hour. The freeways will be empty now, and we'll make really good time. That is, if you don't mind," Robyn said, turning to Peter.

"That's fine," Peter said, surrendering. "I'll just go pack a few things. Juliet, you get the kids' stuff together. How long do you think we'll be gone?"

"A couple of days, no more," Al said. "Don't worry about food and things. Jeanelle's been up at the cabin for the last few days doing some work in the garden. I'm sure she's got the kitchen fully stocked."

"Does she mind my family invading like this?" I asked. "I hate to impose on her time away from the city."

"Not at all. Not at all. She's looking forward to the company. Jeanelle loves kids, and since she's not likely to get a grandchild any time soon, she's delighted to have yours to play with." Robyn rolled her eyes once again and settled herself into a chair to wait for us to pack and get ready.

While Peter put together an overnight case for himself, I packed two or three tons of supplies for the kids. Every time I travel with the children, I remember my days of adventure travel when I saw the sights of Asia and South America weighed down by nothing more than a lightweight backpack and a camera. Nowadays, it takes a semitrailer, two forklifts, and a U-Haul just to get us out for a morning in the park. By narrowing down their wardrobes to just the bare minimum, I managed to fit the kids' clothes, bath supplies, baby bottles, hats, extra shoes, toys, and pills, drops, and bandages for any and all emergencies, into two oversized suitcases. Another bag held a supply of juice boxes, rice cakes, Cheerios, and raisins, with a package of chocolate chip cookies tossed in to guarantee good behavior. They were ready to go.

Miraculously, neither Ruby nor Isaac woke up when we carried them out to the car and loaded them into their car seats. I kissed them on the cheeks, softly enough not to wake them, and watched as they pulled away. I felt a pang in my chest and realized that I'd never been away from Isaac before. This was our first overnight separation. I wondered what my sweet little boy would do when he woke up and found me gone. Have a blast playing cops and robbers with Robyn, probably.

"She won't let the kids near the guns, will she?" I said to Al.

He flashed me the fish eye by way of reply.

Nineteen

By the time I got up the next morning, Al had already made the guest room bed with military precision. I resisted the urge to bounce a quarter off the bedspread and went into the kitchen, where I found him eating a bowl of bran flakes.

"Important for regularity," he said.

"Too much information, Al," I replied and poured myself a cup of coffee. "Are you on the clock?" I asked him.

"Huh?"

"The time clock. Am I paying you your hourly rate as we speak?"

"I don't bill while I'm sleeping or eating. Otherwise, yes, ma'am."

I settled myself on the stool opposite him. "I'd love to have the help, and I'm happy to have the kids and Peter out of harm's way, but I don't think we can afford both you and Robyn."

He swallowed the last mouthful of his cereal and took a noisy gulp of coffee. "How 'bout we work out a swap for services?" he said.

"What do you mean?"

"I provide some muscle on this little project of yours, and the next time I need some advice from a legal eagle, you help me out."

I considered his offer. It had been relatively painless to do Al's legal research. Surely I could offer him those services without impinging too much on car pool and playdates. "Deal," I said, and we shook on it.

We began to draw up a list of all the people with whom I'd had contact over the course of my investigation into Bobby's death. Once we had the names all down on paper, I studied the list.

"Candace," I said.

"Candace?"

"She's the creepiest. She's the one who makes me the most uncomfortable. She's weird, she's unpleasant, and she seems to have built up her relationship with Bobby into a great, unrequited love affair. And she saw Isaac but not Ruby when I tracked her down at her job. It makes sense for her to have threatened my *kid* instead of *kids* because she has no way of knowing I've got two."

"Okay, let's go find Candace."

Twenty

AL and I decided that the benefit of surprise was worth risking the chance that Candace wouldn't be at work. We lucked out. When we walked into the Starbucks across from the Westside Pavilion where she worked, we immediately saw her sitting at one of the little round tables, gripping the hand of a young woman who was weeping into a crumpled tissue. We paused in the doorway and listened.

"Brittany, I know you are doing the right thing. Because I know *you*. You and I have a special bond, a deeper connection than normal people. Our shared abandonment has given us a unique nexus—a union of souls."

The younger woman smiled tearfully at Candace. "You've helped me so much," she hiccuped.

"And you've helped me. We're lost birds, you and I. Two lost birds, clinging to one another in a tumultuous ocean."

"Like a couple of albatrosses," I whispered to Al. He grinned.

We walked over to Candace's table, and I cleared my throat. She looked up at me, clearly irritated at the intrusion, and frowned.

"Yes?" she said.

"It's me, Candace. Juliet Applebaum. Can we talk?"

"I'm very busy right now."

The young woman shook her head. "No, no. That's okay. I've got to go." She stood up and hugged Candace. "I'll E-mail you, okay?"

"I'll be expecting it."

The woman left the café, and Candace turned to me. "I really have to get back to work."

"Take a minute, Candace," Al said, pulling up a chair and sitting down at the table.

"Who's he?" she said to me without looking at Al.

"A colleague. Listen, Candace, we'd like to talk to you a little more about Bobby's death."

The words were barely out of my mouth when she started shaking her head. "I really don't have anything to say. I've moved beyond that whole thing. I'm concentrating on Brittany right now."

"Excuse me?"

"Bobby's gone, and I'm sad, but there are things I need to do. Brittany needs my help. I've got to get back to work." She got up and walked away, ducking under the counter and busying herself at the coffee machine.

Al and I looked at each other, and he raised his eyebrows.

We left the store and stood outside for moment.

"What the hell was that about?" he asked.

"I don't know. It's hard to imagine that she could have just threatened to harm my kids. She didn't seem the slightest bit scared or worried when she saw us."

He shook his head. "More like just not interested."

"She could be faking it."

"She could be."

"So, now what?"

Al rolled his eyes at me. I blushed. "Well, what would you do if you were still a cop?" I asked him.

He shrugged his shoulders and replied, "Interrogate."

"Okay. Let's interrogate her. It's, like, the tiniest problem that we can't arrest her or assert any kind of authority whatsoever, but hey, let's go for it."

"Watch and learn, honey. Watch and learn." He turned and headed back in the door of the café.

I muttered something under my breath about not liking to be called honey, and followed him inside. He ambled up to the counter and leaned on it.

"Candace, we'd like to have just a moment of your time. Can you spare that? For Bobby's sake?" His voice was almost a purr.

She shook her head angrily.

"Let me buy you a coffee," Al insisted. "What kind do you like? A mocha? A latte? How about one of those wonderful frozen things?"

"I hate coffee," she said.

I raised my eyebrows and looked around the café, a veritable shrine to the brew.

"A juice, then," Al said. "And a cookie. For Bobby's sake. Because we all cared about him and want to find out what happened to him."

"Okay, okay," Candace said. She poured herself a glass of milk and took a cookie from the case. "That'll be three dollars and seventeen cents," she said.

Al handed her a five-dollar bill. She ostentatiously dumped the change in the tip cup and ducked under the counter. Then she motioned to us to move to the back of the café. We followed her and sat down at the little table she indicated.

"So, what do you want from me?" she said.

"Just your help. That's all," Al replied in the same honeyed tone with which he'd convinced her to come out from behind her counter.

"How 'bout we start with the most obvious thing. Just a formality really," he said.

"What?"

"Where were you when Bobby was killed?" His voice had suddenly turned stern. Candace flushed, and I held my breath.

"I dunno. Home. I'm always home at night."

"But you don't remember that night specifically?" Al asked.

"No. I mean, why would I? I didn't know he was going to die."

Al turned to me. "Juliet, what was the official time of death?"

I blanched. Had I ever found that out? Al's jaw clenched almost imperceptibly.

"I can prove where I was, no matter what time he died," Candace said.

"Excuse me?" I asked.

"I mean, I can show you where I was."

"At home?" Al asked.

"Yeah, but I mean, I can show you where I was on-line. I'm always on-line."

"All night long?" I asked.

She blushed again. "Yeah. Mostly. Until three or four, at least. That's where I am every night. All you have to do is check the web sites. My posts will all be there. Dated and timed."

"How would we be sure that you didn't just change the date and time on your computer?" Al said.

"Because we can check the posts of the people who replied to her," I said with a sigh. She had seemed such a likely suspect.

"Do you want to look?" Candace said. "I have my laptop." Candace went back behind the counter and pulled out a battered computer carrying case. She plugged the computer into the phone jack and began typing. I spent the next ten minutes bent over the counter at an uncomfortable angle, charting the course of Candace's depressing on-line existence. The women had begun posting messages on various boards at 7 P.M. Her last post was at 5:12 A.M.

"If there's nothing else you want, I'm going to get back to work," she said finally, a victorious note in her voice.

Al and I made our way back to the car. "We'll check the time of death. Maybe it's after 5:12."

"Maybe," Al said, sounding doubtful.

We got in my car and slammed our doors almost in unison. Jiggling the keys in my hand, I said, "Okay, let's start from scratch. What's the first rule of investigating a murder? Look to the family." And then my cell phone rang. It was Michelle.

"I couldn't get the whole Tay-Sachs thing out of my mind," she told me. "It was driving me crazy all night. I mean, of course it's possible that Bobby got the gene from someone with no connection to an at-risk group, but that's just so unlikely."

I agreed with her. "I can't help but feel that if we figure out the source of Bobby's genetic condition, we'll have more of a clue about why he died."

"That's what I was thinking. So, when I got to work this morning, I started searching the medical and genetic databases I work with. You're not going to believe what I found out."

"What?" I said, not doing a very good job of keeping the impatience out of my voice.

"You already know that approximately one in every thirty to thirty-five Ashkenazic Jews, French Canadians, and Louisiana Cajuns is a Tay-Sachs carrier."

"Right."

"Well, it turns out that there is another group with an almost equally high incidence, although for some reason it isn't generally known."

By now I was ready to reach into the phone receiver and yank the words out of her throat by force. "Who?"

"One in every fifty Irish people, or people of exclusively Irish descent, is a Tay-Sachs carrier."

I leaned back in my seat. Major Patrick Sullivan, scion of one of Los Angeles's most prominent Irish Catholic families. Bobby's mother's own husband. He was Bobby's father. But how could he be? I'd considered that possibility more than once but had dismissed it each time. Susan Sullivan herself had told me that there was no way Bobby could have been her husband's child. She said that the only time she'd had sex with her husband in the months before her pregnancy was the time she'd flown out to Japan to meet him on his leave. According to Susan, that had been at least a month before her birth control had failed her with Rueben Nadelman. But, I remembered, she'd also said that Bobby had been born a little early. What if he was, in fact, the product of the Japan leave but had been born a few weeks late, rather than a couple of weeks early?

I thanked Michelle for her research and said a hurried goodbye. Waving off Al's questions, I dialed Susan Sullivan's number. I heaved a sigh of relief when she herself answered the phone.

"It's Juliet Applebaum. Please don't hang up," I said.

"What? What do you want from me? Can't you please leave me alone?" She whined.

"I just have one question for you. Do you remember how much Bobby weighed when he was born?"

"What? Why are you asking me that?"

"Please. It's important. Do you remember?"

"Yes," she whispered, after a pause. "I didn't hold him. I

couldn't bear to. But I asked them whether it was a girl. I'd always wanted a girl. The nurse told me that it was a boy and that he weighed seven pounds seven ounces. I've always remembered because of the drink. You know, seven and seven."

Seven pounds seven ounces. Heavy for a baby born early. Maybe a little small for one born two or three weeks late.

"Susan," I asked. "Did your husband participate in the cystic fibrosis study?"

"No, of course not. He's not a blood relative of my niece."

"Then he never did the genetic screening that you and your sons did?"

"No."

"Susan, is it possible that Bobby was your husband's baby after all? That he wasn't born early but rather a little late, maybe ten months or so after your trip to Japan?"

There was silence on the other end of the line, and then, unexpectedly, the phone went dead.

I turned to Al. "I'll tell you all about it on the way," I said.

"Where are we going?"

"Pacific Palisades."

He shrugged his jacket off and tossed it in the backseat. That was when I noticed the brown leather holster clipped to his belt. I almost told him not to bring the gun, that we wouldn't need it. I don't know why I didn't. Maybe I should have. It's hard to say.

Twenty-one

SALUD answered my ring. She recognized me but didn't seem any more eager to let me in than she had been the last time.

"I go see if Mrs. Susan in," the maid said.

"Podriamos esperar al dentro?" I wheedled. *"Por favor?"* Once again my attempt at conversing in her own language seemed to charm her. She flashed me a silver-capped smile and looked at Al.

"El es un amigo mío," I said, and Al smiled pleasantly.

Salud opened the door and ushered us in, burbling in a Spanish so rapid and thickly accented that I could make out only every couple of words. I nodded and said, *"Sí, claro,"* a few times although I had no idea what I was agreeing with.

She looked at Al and then, in a loud, slow voice, as though

speaking to the infirm, said, "You stay here. I get Mrs. Su-san."

Al and I watched silently as she hurried up the stairs. Al whistled softly as he looked around the marble entryway.

"Classy," he said.

"Old money. Or, as old as it gets around here. Patrick's family made it big in the gold rush and then even bigger in Southern California real estate."

A few moments later, Salud came down the stairs. This time her tread was heavy and slow.

"I am sorry, you go now," she said, motioning us toward the door.

"Que pasa con la señora?" I asked.

"You go now," she said again, refusing to reply in Spanish.

"Tell Mrs. Sullivan that we need to talk to her. It's very important," I insisted.

"She no want to talk to you. She say you go now. So you go."

I looked at Al, and he shrugged his shoulders. Then I started to get angry. I wasn't entirely without sympathy for Susan Sullivan. I could only imagine what the woman was feeling, faced with the possibility that thirty years ago she'd made a horrible mistake. But Bobby Katz was dead, and I wanted answers. I wasn't about to let his birth mother hide out from me. I was getting ready to tell Salud that she should inform Mrs. Susan that she could either talk to me or to the police when the door opened and Matthew Sullivan walked in.

The blond young man was jangling a set of keys in his hand. He wore a buttery-soft, brown leather jacket and those nubbly soled driving shoes that you see in catalogues but nobody ever buys. Nobody outside of a Connecticut country club, that is. His face stiffened when he saw me, and then he smiled politely.

"Can I help you? Juliet, is it? My mother's friend from the library benefit."

"Er, right. The library benefit. I'm just here to talk to your mother for a moment."

"Mr. Matthew, Mrs. Susan say she no want to see the lady. She say the lady should go home," Salud insisted.

The blond man shrugged his shoulders. "I'm afraid my mother is busy, Mrs. Applebaum. You'll have to come back some other time."

"Matthew, I don't know your mother from the library. I need to speak to her about something personal and urgent. Why don't you go upstairs and tell your mother that if she won't talk to me, I'm going to have no choice but to go to the police with what I know."

His face blanched. "What are you talking about?" he said.

"It's personal. Just tell her."

He looked over at Al. "Who's that? Are you a cop?" His voice was hoarse and worried.

"I'm a colleague of Ms. Applebaum's," Al said. "Go tell your mother that we'd like a few words. If you don't mind." Al had perfected his calm but firm cop's voice. Matthew looked for a moment like he was about to follow the gently given instruction. At that moment, the door opened again, and Patrick Sullivan walked into the house.

"Hello?" he said in a questioning voice. "What's going on here?"

His son turned beet red and began to mumble something unintelligible.

"Mr. Patrick, Mrs. Susan say she no want to talk to these people, but they no leaving," Salud said.

"Can I help you?" His voice was cold and foreboding.

For a brief second, I considered spilling the story to him, Susan's feelings be damned, but I couldn't bring myself to completely destroy the life she was so intent on keeping intact and undisturbed.

"We were just leaving," I said and motioned to Al to follow.

Susan's husband waved to his son. "Please see them out," he said.

Matthew jerked the door open, and Al and I filed through. As I walked by the young man, I reached into my pocket, pulled out a business card, and pressed it into his trembling hand. In a low, hurried voice meant for his ears only, I said, "This has my cell phone number on it. Tell your mom that she might be able to catch us on our way to the police station."

We'd parked the car on the circular driveway right in front of the house. As we pulled around to leave, Al said, "Well, so much for that."

"Do you think she's just having some kind of hysterical breakdown at the thought of having given up her husband's baby, or do you think she knows something about Bobby's death?"

He shrugged his shoulders.

"Maybe she killed him, and she's having a hysterical breakdown because she just realized that she killed not just her own son, but her husband's, too," I said.

"Maybe who Bobby's father is has nothing at all to do with his death."

I hit the brakes and turned to Al. "You were the one who was so big on the no-coincidences theory!"

He shrugged his shoulders, and I shook my head at him. Before I stepped on the gas, I looked back up the long drive-way through my rearview mirror. A silver Audi TT and a gold Lexus coupe were parked around the side of the house in front of the three-car garage. Neither had been there when we'd arrived. I pulled into the street and headed toward Sunset Boulevard. Suddenly, I remembered the little sports car that had zipped by me on the PCH the last time I'd visited Susan Sullivan. I remembered the racing car that the boys said they'd seen when Peter's BMW had been vandal-ized. I pulled over to the side of the road with a screech and turned to Al.

"That's the car," I said.

Al raised his eyebrows questioningly, and I reminded him about the boys and described the car that had almost rear-ended me.

"The Audi. It's got to be the Audi."

Al wasn't convinced. "It's possible. But if we call the de-tectives with nothing more than the possibility that the rac-ing car the kids described could have been maybe the same Audi that blew by you on the highway and that might maybe be the same Audi that's in this driveway, even though thousands of those cars are floating around the city right now, they're going to laugh in our faces."

I knew he was right. "Well then, let's get them something more than that."

He looked at me for a moment as if trying to figure out whether I was determined or foolhardy or both. Then he patted the gun strapped to his waist. "All right. Let's."

Twenty-two

Aᴛ first, no one answered our ring. Then I leaned on the bell. After a couple of cacophonous moments, Patrick Sullivan wrenched the door open and glared at us.

"Look here, I've had about as much as I'm willing to take of you. My wife doesn't want to see you. Get away from my front door and off of my property before I call the police." He hunched over into my face and spoke through gritted teeth. I felt a thin spray of spittle and didn't wipe my cheek, although I desperately wanted to.

"Mr. Sullivan, my friend Bobby Katz is dead. He was shot in the head, and I think your wife knows something about how and why he was killed. And, frankly, I'm betting you or your son Matthew knows, too."

His eyes narrowed. "What are you talking about?" I

couldn't tell if his ignorance was real or feigned.

"Mr. Sullivan, if you want to call the police, by all means go ahead and do so. I'm sure they'd be interested in exploring your family's involvement in Bobby's death. Alternatively, you could let us in and help us figure out what may well be an innocent explanation for all this."

Patrick Sullivan stared at me, his face inscrutable. Then, suddenly, he stretched out his arm and opened the door wide. "Come in," he said.

He led us through the circular entry hall and into the living room. We stood on the crimson Chinese carpet in the middle of the room. He didn't invite us to sit down.

"Wait here. I'll get my wife," he said and left us, clicking the door shut behind him.

Al rocked back and forth on his heels. I paced nervously.

"Do you have *any* idea what you're going to say when he drags the woman down here to talk to you?" Al asked.

I scowled at him. "More or less. Have some faith."

We both turned to the door when it opened, expecting to see Susan Sullivan. Her son Matthew stood there instead. He was pale and sweaty, and his breath came in shallow gasps, audible across the room. He looked like he'd been running or crying.

"Get out! Get out of here!" He tried to shout, but his voice cracked and came out an awkward squeal.

"We're here to talk to your mother, Matthew," I said.

"Get out!" This time he managed the yell.

I could see Al firming up his stance out of the corner of my eye. His feet were planted shoulder-width apart, and he'd assumed a barely detectable crouch. He was ready to spring at the young man if he needed to.

"Hey, Matthew," I said in a conversational tone. "Is that your Audi or your dad's?"

His face turned beet red, and he lunged at me. Al, moving more quickly than a man of his age has any right to, stepped between us. He grabbed Matthew around the shoulders with one arm and swung him away from me. Matthew wiggled frantically in his grip. Before I could make it across the room to the grappling men, Matthew had somehow managed to yank one arm free of Al's, and he was punching wildly. The two men slipped on the edge of the carpet and fell to the ground with a thud. I saw Al's hand fumbling with his holster as I ran to help him subdue Matthew. I had just reached the two when I heard a pop like a piece of wood snapping in two. Suddenly, Matthew was pointing the gun at Al, who knelt, hunched over, holding his right hand against his chest. His index finger was bent at an unnatural angle, and he groaned.

"Get over there with him," Matthew said, swinging the gun in my direction. It wobbled in his trembling hand, and I was terrified that he would accidentally pull the trigger. I walked quickly over to Al and helped him to his feet. We backed away from Matthew. Al and I both stared at the gun. Matthew followed our gaze and suddenly pulled back the safety.

"I can shoot it now," he said, and he made a sound halfway between a giggle and a groan. Sweat was pouring freely down his forehead, and he hitched up his shoulder to wipe it away. At that moment, his parents walked into the room. Susan gave a strangled cry and began to run to her son, but Patrick yanked her back.

"Matthew! What the hell do you think you're doing? Put that gun down!" Patrick bellowed.

Matthew's back was to the door, and he turned slowly, keeping the gun aimed at Al and me.

"You go stand with them, too," he said, the words hissing from his throat.

"What the devil—" his father began.

"Do it!" he shrieked, and the Sullivans joined us where we stood, backed against the long sofa.

"Sit," he said, his voice almost gleeful, as though he was relishing the opportunity to force us to comply. Patrick did not seem a man who took orders willingly, certainly not from his son. It was obviously an unusual pleasure for Matthew to feel power over his father.

Al, Susan, and I sat, but Patrick remained standing. "Sit down, Dad."

"Look here, Matthew. This is ridiculous. Hand me the gun."

"No."

Patrick took a step forward. "Come on, son. Give me that gun."

"I'll shoot. I will. Stop!" The young man's teeth were gritted shut as he tried to keep his voice from quavering. Patrick kept moving forward, and Matthew suddenly swung the gun in the direction of his mother.

"I'll shoot her!" he screamed. And his father stopped stock-still. Susan whimpered.

"Shut up!" her son screamed at her. "This is your fault. All of it. You're a . . . a slut! That's what you are. You're a whore!"

The woman's chest rose and fell with her sobs. Matthew kept talking. "I knew you'd done it. I knew it as soon as the genetic counselor told me I had that Jew disease."

"Son, son, what are you saying?" Patrick's voice had lost its authoritative swagger. He sounded afraid.

"It's not what you think, Matthew," I said calmly and slowly. Everyone looked at me except Al, who kept his eyes fixed on the gun in Matthew's hand.

"What do *you* know?" Matthew snarled.

"You tested positive for Tay-Sachs, right? You're a carrier?"

"No! You're not. You can't be," Susan cried. "You said you weren't. And you can't be."

"I lied! Of course I lied. You and P. J. each said you didn't have any of the three diseases. And then Dad said of course you didn't because Sullivans are a strong breed. How the hell was I supposed to tell you that I had it? How? Particularly since I know what it means!"

"You *don't* know, Matthew. You're making a mistake," I said.

"What are you talking about?" Patrick said. "Matthew, Susan, what the hell is she talking about?"

I didn't reply to Patrick. I kept talking to Matthew quietly but firmly. "Bobby got in touch with you, didn't he?"

The young man nodded. "He said he was my brother. He asked me to meet him, and I did. He told me that she didn't want to have anything to do with him but that he hoped I might. He told me about the Tay-Sachs, and that's when I knew I had to do it."

My chest tightened, and I could feel my eyes begin to burn as tears collected in them. "Matthew, did you hurt Bobby?" I asked in a soft, gentle voice.

"I had to," he whined.

I could hear Susan's harsh, ragged sobs and willed her silently to keep her mouth shut. Patrick seemed stunned and unable to speak.

"I had to," he repeated. "He wasn't going to leave it alone. He wasn't going to go away. He was going to make her tell Dad, and then Dad would find out about me. I couldn't let that happen. I couldn't let that happen." He turned to his father. "I know you hate me. I know you're just looking for a good reason to cut me off. You want to throw me out, but you don't think you can, right? Right?"

This time it was Patrick who sobbed. I turned to look at him, expecting to see him reduced to tears. His eyes were absolutely dry.

"You were afraid that if Bobby forced your mother to tell your father about him, then Patrick would find out about you, too?" I asked, again keeping my voice low and calm.

He nodded.

I continued. "You're afraid that you're not your father's son, aren't you?"

"I'm *not* his son. She had an affair. She had an affair, and she got pregnant, and she had Bobby and gave him away. And then she kept on seeing the guy, and she had me. I

don't know why she didn't give me up, too." He stared at
Susan and cried, "Why did you keep me? Why didn't you
give me away like you gave away my brother?"

Susan didn't answer. She had her hands clasped over her
mouth, and she rocked back and forth, moaning. Patrick
stared at his wife, rage and disgust warring on his face.

"You're wrong, Matthew. You *are* your father's son. And
so was Bobby. Your mother did have an affair while your
father was in Vietnam, and she did give Bobby up for adoption, but you're wrong about the rest, Matthew."

Matthew shook his head furiously, but his eyes narrowed
as he looked at me.

"Bobby didn't come from the affair your mother had.
Bobby is Patrick's son, too. Just like you are. Tay-Sachs
doesn't just affect Jews, Matthew. Anyone can have it. Anyone, especially the Irish. It's almost as common in the Irish
population as in the Jewish. You inherited the Tay-Sachs
from your father."

"What?" the young man whispered. "What?"

"Patrick *is* your father, Matthew. And he was Bobby's."

"No. No he's not. Is he? Is he?" The young man shrieked,
first at me and then at his mother.

"I don't know, I don't know," Susan whispered.

At that moment we all heard the faint sounds of sirens.
We stiffened as they grew closer and closer. Matthew's arm
began to sink to his side so slowly that it was at first almost
imperceptible. Al and I both rose to our feet, also slowly.
Matthew said nothing, he just continued to lower his arm.
I stepped to one side of him and Al to the other. Al reached

out his hand and carefully and deliberately removed the gun from Matthew's now limp palm. He slipped it back into the holster attached to his belt. The police found us thus, Al with the gun securely clipped in its place, Matthew trembling, just barely managing to keep to his feet, and Susan and Patrick sitting next to each other on their lovely and expensive sofa, frozen in despair.

Twenty-three

THE police kept us there for quite a while. I'm sure it was Al's status as a retired member of the LAPD that finally convinced them that it was safe to take our names and telephone numbers and let us go on our way. We drove in silence down Sunset Boulevard. I wasn't thinking about what had happened so much as I was trying to figure out the best way to break the news to Bobby's fiancée and his family. I knew the police would inform them, but that could take some time, and I certainly owed it to Betsy and Michelle to tell them myself. I didn't realize how distraught Al was until he cleared his throat. I looked over at him sitting in the passenger seat. His face was blotchy under a sheen of sweat.

"Are you okay?" I said. "What's wrong? Are you feeling all right? Should I pull over?"

He shook his head and cleared his throat once again.

"I'm . . . I'm very sorry. Truly. And I'll understand if you don't want to partner with me anymore."

I took a quick right into the parking lot of a big box store and pulled the car into a spot. I turned off the engine and turned to face him. Looking him full in the eye I said, "What the hell are you talking about?" Although I knew. Of course I knew.

"My gun. I let that kid get hold of my gun. You could have been killed. I let him overpower me, and I endangered both our lives."

To a man who had always been as physically powerful as Al, the vulnerability that comes with age must be devastating. How impossibly painful it is to acknowledge that you are no longer able to protect yourself and others, when that has always been your primary occupation, the source of your identity. If your physical strength is one of your paramount skills, what must it feel like when that begins to go?

I'd often wondered how it was that Al made the transition from law enforcement to defense investigation so easily. It had never seemed to bother him that his job was no longer to protect and defend but rather to work toward the release of those who he'd once been so committed to incarcerating. Sitting next to him in the car, I understood that it had only seemed to come naturally to him. Perhaps the job of defense investigator had enough of the trappings of the police—he investigated, he searched, sometimes at least, for truth—that he could feel like he was still in the business of protecting people. At the moment when Matthew wrenched the gun from his hand, Al must suddenly have confronted the fact that not only was his job no longer to protect the public, but he was no longer even able to protect himself and those he cared about in the way he once had.

"You didn't *let* him get your gun," I said. "You didn't let him do anything."

Al shook his head and knotted his old man's hands, gnarled like tree branches, in his lap. His index finger was swollen and red. There was something very wrong with it.

I reached out my own hand and rested it ever so gently on his. He flinched slightly. "Al, listen to me. I know this is hard. I know twenty years ago, hell, even ten years ago, Matthew would never have gotten your gun away from you—"

Al grunted. "He should never have been able to lay a hand on my gun. Not then, and not now. Never."

"Al, the guy's in his early twenties. He's strong and young and out of his mind. Crazy people are capable of amazing feats of strength; you know that. He was desperate, and he got lucky. I mean, look at your hand! He snapped your finger! There's no way you could have held on to the gun."

Al stared at his swollen finger and gave it an angry shake. He immediately winced in pain.

"I've got to get you to a doctor to have that that taken care of. It looks excruciating."

He looked for a moment like he was going to object, then he shrugged. "Don't worry. I'll get it looked at. Some bodyguard, huh?"

"You're not my bodyguard. You're my *partner*."

He raised his eyebrows at me. I waved him off. "Look, I want to break this news to Michelle and Betsy in person. You coming?" I asked. He nodded. "Should we stop at an emergency room?"

"Let's do it later," Al said. "If we go now, we'll be there all day waiting for them to deal first with the coke-head gang-bangers bleeding to death."

That's my buddy Al, always able to toss a slur even in the midst of exquisite agony.

Before I pulled out of the parking lot, I handed him my cell phone and asked him to call Big Bear and let everyone know that the police had Matthew in custody and that the kids were no longer in danger. Al spoke quickly to Jeannelle—Peter and Robyn had taken the kids out for a hike—and then I called Michelle. I tracked her down at her lab. I didn't want to tell her on the phone, so I asked her if we could come see her.

As soon as Michelle met Al and me in the lobby of her building, she ushered us back through the double doors marked Authorized Personnel Only to a small office kitchenette. She pulled a first aid kit out of a cupboard and held out her hand for Al's. With a quick snap, she'd straightened out his finger. He'd winced briefly, but by the time she'd taped it to a tongue depressor, he was smiling.

"Thank you, dear. You just saved me about three hours and three hundred bucks at the ER."

She said, "It was just dislocated, but I'm happy to oblige. Actually, I like being reminded that I'm also a real doctor now and again."

Al and I took Michelle up on her offer of coffee, and we sat at the Formica table in the sterile little kitchenette and told her how her brother had died. She cried, but it seemed as much with relief as sorrow. Knowing that Bobby hadn't killed himself, and knowing why Matthew had murdered him, gave her some sense of peace. More, certainly, than she'd had before.

"It just seems so pointless," she sighed, wiping tears from her eyes.

"It almost always is, in my experience," I said. "People never kill each other for very good reasons. It's usually about love, or jealousy, or some horrible misunderstanding. And it never feels justified to those left behind."

Michelle asked me to leave it to her to tell her family, and I was only too happy to agree. After my recent conversation with her father, I'd been dreading seeing him again. And we still had to break the news to Betsy.

I called Betsy from the car but got a busy signal, so we just headed over to Hollywood.

Betsy's door was opened by the same man who had been there when last I'd seen her. He had a cigarette clenched in his teeth, and he squinted his eyes against the smoke curling from the end. He was holding a roll of packing tape in one hand and a thick magic marker in the other.

"Yes?" he said. "Oh, right. The detective girl."

Al nudged me in the side with his elbow, but I ignored him. "I'm a lawyer, actually. Is Betsy around?"

Roy took the cigarette out of his mouth and ground it out in a little white saucer that looked like it had been serving as his ashtray for quite a while. "Nobody told you?" he said.

"Nobody told me what?"

"About Betsy?"

My stomach knotted in dread. "What happened?" I asked.

"Betsy had a positive urine test. Her probation officer had her arrested."

I wasn't surprised. I looked around the shambles of the living room. Cardboard boxes rested on every available surface.

"You're packing?" I asked.

"She asked me to. Her lawyer told her she's looking at a few months in county, at the minimum. Since she's getting evicted at the end of the month, she asked me to take care of her stuff for her. I'm putting it all into storage."

"She's going to jail?" I asked. "Not into a drug treatment facility?"

He nodded. "Sick, isn't it? I mean, the woman has a disease, but instead of giving her the medicine and therapy she needs, they throw her in jail. Where, incidentally, she'll be able to get as much crank as her little heart desires."

I shook my head. "Ridiculous."

I could feel Al aching to put his two cents into the conversation, surely to comment on how using drugs is against the law and people who break the law deserve to go to jail, but I silenced him with a glare. The last thing I was interested in at the moment was one of our trademark political debates.

"Are you planning on visiting her?" I asked.

"Once they let me, yeah, I will."

I told him what had happened and asked him if he would be willing to pass word on to Betsy. I also promised that I'd go to county jail to visit her.

I guess I wasn't surprised that Betsy hadn't managed to stay sober. Most addicts don't. Drug addiction is a complicated thing. It seems to take some remarkable combination of support, security, and will to kick the habit. And even with all that to help them, many people still end up locked into a cycle of using that destroys them and those around them. I hoped Betsy would survive her months in county and come out with the strength and desire to try again. I wasn't about to lay any money on it, though.

Twenty-four

AL and I drove down La Brea toward my house in silence. Finally, as I pulled in the driveway, I said, "Okay, I'll do it."

He looked at me, puzzled. "Do what?"

"Go into business with you. But in a really limited way."

"Go on."

"First of all, I need completely flexible hours. I mean, I've got to be able to pick Ruby up at school, take care of Isaac, take the kids to playdates. All that."

He shrugged. "That's fine by me. Work when you want to work."

"And I don't want to commit to a firm number of hours or anything like that. If you need some legal research done, and I'm free, then I'll do it. But I can't promise anything."

"What an attractive offer," he said.

"Those are my terms. I don't really want to go back to work, anyway. I'm a stay-at-home mom. I'm happy that way."

"Sure you are."

I decided to ignore that. "How are you going to pay me?"

"I'm not."

"What?"

"I'm not going to pay you. The clients will pay you. If I've got work for you, and you can fit me into your busy schedule, then you'll do the work and we'll bill the client. Whatever they pay me for your time, I'll give to you."

"Okay. That sounds fair. Oh, and one more thing."

"What?"

"I'm not carrying a gun. Ever."

"We'll see about that."

"I'm serious, Al."

"Okay, okay."

"Do we have a deal?"

"Yes, I believe we do."

We shook on it.

After Al went home, it occurred to me that it might be a good idea to have some welcome-home presents waiting for the kids. Actually, the most important person to reward was probably Peter. I headed out to the Toys "R" Us on La Cienega, across from the Beverly Center, and meandered up and down the aisles for a while. I found a truly disgusting doll for Ruby that would pee after drinking a bottle and poop after being fed a special powdered pap (sold separately). She would love it. I picked out a Johnny Lightning Speed

Racer Mach 5 for Peter. As for Isaac, it didn't take me long to find the perfect gift. When I got home, I wrapped everything in some Chanukah paper I found under my bed and sat down at the kitchen table to wait.

It took them quite a while to make it down from Big Bear—it had snowed that morning—and, finally, I was bored enough to whip up a batch of chocolate chip cookies. I had eaten my way through half the cookie dough and most of the cookies, too, when I heard the car pull into the driveway. I ran down the back stairs and greeted them as they tumbled out. The kids were squealing and ruddy-cheeked from their adventures in the snow. Peter looked exhausted and very happy to be home. We hugged, kissed, and staggered up the stairs with all their bags and boxes.

Sitting on the floor in the living room, my husband and I cuddled as Ruby and Isaac tore the wrapping paper off their presents.

"You okay?" Peter asked.

"Now I am," I said, kissing him on the cheek.

Suddenly, Isaac screamed in delight. "A gun! A real gun! A gun! A gun! A gun!"

"A gun?" Peter was obviously shocked.

"A purple water pistol," I said.

"Don't we have a rule against guns?"

"Relax," I said. I picked my son up onto my lap and kissed him on his round, soft cheek. "Isaac and I know it's just pretend. Right, Isaac?" He took aim at me with the purple pistol, right between the eyes, and squeezed off a round, point-blank.

"Pow," Isaac said. "You're dead."